THE CHUPACABRA FILES

VICTOR DIAMANTE

THE CHUPACABRA FILES Copyright ©2022
Line By Lion Publications
www.pixelandpen.studio

ISBN: 9781948807289

Cover Art:Thomas Lamkin Jr and Victor Diamante.
Editing By Ian Jedlica

To those who have been beyond the brink and came back to tell the tale.

TOP

SECRET

CLASSIFIED

NOT FOR
DISSEMINATION

I don't know how you got your hands on this file but you better stop reading it. This is your last warning!!!!!

Fine. You are obviously going to keep reading this but you should know this; this warning is for your own protection. Reading this report will put your life in certain danger by the fact that you will be injecting forbidden and highly-classified intelligence into your unauthorized brain.

Should you ever be asked, questioned, debriefed, interrogated, subjected to a lie-detector or God forbid tortured for intelligence extraction, you will not be able to conceal the knowledge you are foolishly and needlessly pursuing at your own peril.

Good luck

...

Origin of species Caprae Quae Stirpibus AKA "Chupacabras"

FILE INVENTORY

FILE 1

Welcome to the Government

THE world changes at an astounding rate. But we are in it. We do not, we cannot, notice the supersonic speed at which society evolves or devolves. But when you remove yourself from society for a substantial period of time, you notice the change whether you like it or not.

I first realized this phenomenon when I enlisted in the United States Marine Corps. Within the first 24 hours at Marine Corps Recruit Depot (MCRD) San Diego I realized how desperately separated I was from society.

I remember...

This recruit was rushed along with 100 other bald-headed recruits from our platoon into the largest hall this recruit had ever existed in. It was like a baseball stadium had morphed into a carpeted auditorium that thought it was a non-denominational church. This recruit felt like an amoeba crawling on the floor of the Grand Canyon.

In the hall were hundreds, thousands of other recruits being mindlessly commanded to "Stand up! No. Sit Down! I said stand up! Sit down now!" After each command, these recruits had to yell "Aye Aye Sir!" The drill instructors (DIs) commanded. "Louder!" "Louder Aye Sir!" These recruits destroyed these recruits' own weakling vocal cords in a matter of days. Thousands and thousands of recruits being controlled and driven mad in deafening noise to instill "instant obedience to orders Sir!"

Then the DIs gave one final command. "Sit!" These recruits' response was bellowed in chaos but echoed in silence "Sit aye, Sir."

The heel clicks of a general ricocheted off the wooden walls of the cathedral/stadium as he walked in. His words were few. As a Marine, he needed no microphone.

"At O-six hundred this morning, local time, Saddam Hussein, Prime Minister of Iraq invaded Saudi Arabia, one of our closest allies in the Middle East, deploying thousands of troops and tanks in a ground war killing at least 5 thousand civilians within two hours. They are our friends. We are Marines. As of this moment, I, General (I forgot his name) designate every single one of you recruits as combat infantry Marines to bring down this mad man until Iraq is once again a free nation! You should be proud. You're all going to be heroes."

Yelps cried out from the far corners of the hall from recruits who had enlisted only to be mechanic Marines. Muffled cries escaped the quivering lips of former administrative Marines who thought they'd only be doing paperwork for the next four years.

"You are about to endure the toughest four months of your life here at MCRD San Diego because in four months and one day you will all be fighting AmVictora's next war and many of you will die glorious deaths in combat and will not come back alive if you come back at all! Gentlemen, carry on."

Now, full-on weeping was erupting from everywhere as men were learning their fates had been sealed. These recruits had all entered during a time of peace but had just learned that peace had turned into hell.

This recruit had enlisted as a 4300 designation, Public Affairs option. So, this recruit was one of those who had not joined for the glory of war. Other original infantry Marines were not crying, they were practically glowing.

Then a thought entered this recruit's brain-housing group. Is this real? What if they are messing with these recruits to exhibit the gravity of the decision these recruits had all made. This recruit did not cry. This recruit saw other recruits next to this recruit weeping like children. But was it real? The government wouldn't lie to us. But what if they said it was for a really good reason? There was no way to tell. These recruits were cut off from the world. No TV. No Radio. No newspapers. Cell phones and the Internet itself hadn't even been invented yet; not officially. These recruits might as well have been on the face of Mars. We were as close to the world as the world was to Betelgeuse.

In the end, it all turned out to be a hoax; A mind game. One of many mind games the Marine Corps played on us. I remember one DI would always tell us, "I got more games than Milton Bradley, boy." But these games were not played for fun. They were played for the business of war. I get it. I ain't mad at the Corps. I love the Corps. It made me who I am today; the bad and the good.

The day before I left for boot camp, I wrote a letter to myself. A letter telling me to remain a poet. To love art. To make art. Make love. Love life. Live free. And above all, do not change.

The day I got home from boot camp, I read it. I laughed because of that first day in the cathedral; the mind games, the training, the indoctrination, all of it. It changed me. The world had changed but because I was not in it, I noticed.

FILE 2

Notoriety

THE first thing I noticed about the world when I graduated from boot camp and went back into the world was the colors. The world is so vibrant with neon rainbow colors all around us. We have created a world that is so bright and multicolored, our brains have to dull them down to a manageable level.

The only colors we saw for four long months were green, black and tan and all shades therein. But driving outside the MCRD the colors bombarded my eyes like red, blue and green kamikazes ramming into my face and brain. It was gorgeous.

After that, the billboards on the hills had all changed. The clothes people were wearing. The radio was playing all new music. At home, all the TV shows and movies were things I hadn't even conceived were happening.

The thing I remember the most though was the one thing the entire world was talking about and I had no idea what the heck it was. I had ten days to catch up on the current pulse of society as I was on leave and soon would be back at Marine Combat Training which is like part two of boot camp.

While marveling at the new world into which I had emerged, my sisters asked me if I had heard about chupacabra.

"Chupa what?" I asked.

"Chupacabra."

"What the heck is a chupacabra?"

"You haven't heard about chupacabra? Damn dude, everyone is talking about him."

"Well, what the heck is it?"

"It's this, like this monster thing that goes around killing goats."

"Killing goats? What the heck? Why would anything kill something so delicious?" I said. "Besides, what have goats ever done to deserve that anyway?"

"I don't know dude," said my eldest sister. "It's just this thing that people are seeing everywhere. There's been sightings all along the border and especially near ranches and in the deserts. Someone said they even found one in Texas."

"What the hell is a *cabra* anyway?" I asked.

"It's a goat," said my Mom.

"So, what? We got tired of hating on Bigfoot and the Loch Ness Monster and had to make our own Mexican version? This is stupid. People are stupid," I said.

"No dude, it's real!" said my sister. "They even showed one on the news the other day and people say it looks disgusting."

"They showed it on the news?" I asked.

Remember, back then, there was no internet or social media. There were traditional media and the Dewey Decimal system; that's pretty much it. It was also before "fake news." There was always the Enquirer and other rags for entertainment, but the news was something you could actually trust. We didn't know of right-wing, left-wing, or politically leaning news outlets. Only that if the news said it, it had to be real.

"Did *you* see it on the news?" I asked.

"Mmm. Well. No. I didn't. But I heard that they actually showed one."

"Well, what does it look like?" I asked.

"Like an alien. But it has giant red eyes, and it has spikes coming out of its back," said my sister.

"So… basically, it's an alien?" I declared.

"Who knows dude but people are scared," she said.

"Of a Mexican version of Bigfoot? Okay," I laughed.

I dismissed it as public stupidity. An example of people willing to believe anything as long as it was fun to think about. But as the days went on, I was startled to see that this Chupa, whatever the hell, was everywhere.

Because I had a little spending money now, I took my mom shopping and as we were looking around the Chino stores on Mission and Ajo where the Fry's used to be, I saw a freaking chupacabra T-shirt; Then another and another. Outside the store, some Mexican dude was hocking bootleg chupacabra movies. And I don't mean many copies of the same movie. I mean completely different movies all about chupacabra.

"Chupacabra versus Las Momias de Guanajuato," "Chupacabra versus Espiderman," "Chupacabra does New York," and so on. They even had a workout video called "Sudando con el Chupis," or "Sweating with Chupis," (short for chupacabra). On that cover, they featured chupacabra wearing a pink sweatband and curling some purple hand-weights surrounded by vivacious ladies. Classic Mexican culture.

On the way home, I was tuning through the radio. No. Not XM Radio or Bluetooth connected music streaming through my cell phone, I mean good old-fashioned radio waves.

"Y ahora, tenemos la canción más pedida del dia, 'La Cumbia del Chupacaaaaaaaabraaaaaaaassss.' Aqui, nomas en La Caliiiieeeeeennnnnte." Then the song started. "Vamos, vamos, vamos a bailar con chupacabra. Todos, todos, todos a gozar con chupacabras..." I could not believe it. What the hell had happened to the world? Does the world always change this fast? Does the world always change this much? I know now that it does. I didn't know that people can't help but change with the times. We are helpless and are always swept away with the currents of time.

As time passed, so did the fad of chupacabra. Like parachute pants, the Rubik's Cube, stonewashed jeans, quebradita, Westerns and surf music passed on, so too, did chupacabra.

FILE 3

The General

FIFTEEN years, three jobs, two kids, an ex-wife, a new one, a new house, and a new career later, I was working at the Tucson Sector Border Patrol Headquarters in the Communications Division in Tucson, AZ which all-in-all was a certified miracle. God Himself moved His hand through what we know as space and time and placed me where he needed me.

I had a lot of bad times, but more good times in the Corps. Either way, it seemed all of my experiences in ten years in the Marine Corps, especially photography, marketing, media, public relations and hard work and adversity had all been preparation just to work in Public Affairs for the Border Patrol as a Public Information Officer (PIO).

One of the best parts of that job was taking media, dignitaries, and all manner of VIPs on ride-alongs to the desert where they could see what a U.S. Border Patrol Agent actually does in the field. Since I hailed from the Ajo Station, I was in charge of the West Desert corridor, which at that time, was the busiest smuggling corridor in the country. We faced the daily task of targeting, identifying and interdicting the Mexican Cartel's main supply lines of drugs and humans.

I personally gave ride-alongs to people from Fox News, CNN, The New York Times, all the major local and state media outlets and media from all over the world. I met people from Australia, Japan, Germany, Mexico, the UK, the Netherlands, Costa Rica, Spain, Israel and more. But the ride-along I remember the most was the one I gave to a military general from Puerto Rico. (I just can't remember his name.)

I remember his face. He was of very light complexion, about 5'11" and very muscular. I even thought he could have been an amateur bodybuilder or weightlifter. He had a thin, almost blond mustache.

When he spoke English, he spoke it properly but elementary and with a hard Spanish accent. He always made his voice sound deeper than it was. When he spoke Spanish, he spoke at a very educated level. He almost sang his words, like an old Spanish song.

In contrast, my Spanish is more elementary but still proper. My English, on the other hand, is proper and very clear; without an accent. I never intended it that way, it's just how I turned out. I remember in middle school when I had met real cholos for the very first time. They would make fun of me because I never said 'homes,' 'ese' or 'Si, heck yeah homie.' At least not seriously. They said I spoke like a white boy. I told them speaking white and speaking intelligently is not the same thing. "There is a difference." I was a bit arrogant but I never apologized for the way I spoke.

After muddling through the formalities of English for the first few awkward minutes at HQ, (headquarters), I started speaking Spanish; real Spanish; as real as my English. He seemed surprised.

"Bough!" he blurted. "I thought you were a coconut," he jovially confessed.

"I get that a lot," I laughed.

"No! But after hearing you speak Spanish, I'm impressed. I'll never think that of you again," he said.

"Hmm. Thanks, General," I laughed.

Although it seemed nothing could ever bother such a man, I could tell he also felt relief. He could be himself. He no longer had to lower his voice or raise his guard. His real voice was a bit higher but still very loud and strong; like a trumpet.

He wore tan, military fatigues; no blingy insignia or name tapes so as not to give away his identity or position to the unsuspecting public. My eye of course always looked for a concealed weapon. Even though at first, he was trying to hide it, after a while, he let his guard down just enough for me to catch a glimpse of a shiny pistol, probably a Glock or a 9 mil. I never thought he would have to use it, though. I had my M4 at vehicle standby if the need ever arose. Either way, I was fine with it. After all, he was extremely vetted.

We got into our BP Suburban and headed west. We departed Tucson three hours before sundown as I always did. This allows for travel and lets us get the lay of the land before the darkness drops.

I was told by HQ that in his official request through the State Department, he requested to see the challenges the Border Patrol faces on the U.S./Mexico Border and apply what he learned in the West Desert to the security of Puerto Rico (PR).

Although PR is an island unto itself, only 70 miles to its west is the island of Hispaniola; half Dominican Republic (DR) and half Haiti. Both are desperate countries engulfed in poverty. DR is bad but Haiti is much, much worse. The people of Hispaniola often plunge into the open sea on a journey that might lead them to the refuge of Puerto Rico or to the shores of the next life. Either way, they were coming to PR, the good, the bad and the ugly.

The loving and the innocent say, "Let them come! They are looking for a better life." Yet the hard lessons of the border have taught me that every single person must be vetted. Unseen evil often sleeps beneath a peaceful smile; waiting to slip through a crack to attack an easier target. So, I believe in the General's mission. I will help him. I felt proud to be the one chosen to take him to the West Desert.

We spoke endlessly about border security, technology, personnel and infrastructure. I knew the five or six-hour spiel almost like a script, but it was all true. We had extensive conversations on biometrics collections; DNA, fingerprinting, facial recognition, retinal scanners and all manner of confirming who a person is, not who they claim to be.

I told him about the time I spent at least 30 minutes talking and laughing with a sweet, older woman as I processed her in our detention facility in Ajo, AZ. I was sure she had been apprehended by some silly mistake. She spoke about her children and her grandchildren and how much she missed them. I assured her that we would get this whole mess cleared up in no time and at the very least, she would be back with her grandchildren to make them warm tortillas in no time.

After we pulled her rap sheet, it revealed she was a convicted felon with charges racking all the way from drug smuggling to kidnapping, extortion, money laundering and even assault with a deadly weapon. She was what was known as a "veterana." She was a very bad person but I was fooled by her exterior. I never knew what ominous plans were churning behind her seemingly warm, brown eyes.

She was wanted by the U.S. Marshals and had several warrants for her arrest. We notified them and before the sun came up, they had her in custody; handcuffed behind her back. They were transferring her to federal prison to be locked away for many years for her heinous crimes.

I remember, before they took her away, she looked back at me, over her handcuffs and smiled. Evil emanated from her eyes and from her dirty teeth. She was laughing at me. Even though she was the one who was literally chained up, she felt pride that her act had fooled me. After that, I never assumed anyone was good. I tried not to assume they were bad either; only that I had apprehended a person and that biometrics, immune to trickery, would determine their path.

The General nodded that he understood. I believed him. We pressed on. We made one final stop in Three Points, AZ for water, snacks or any other necessities. We grabbed water and some munchies for the trip.

"This is the point of no return," I laughingly said to the General. "If you have any phone calls or texts you want to send out, this is your last chance. After here, there is no cell phone service."

"No. All notifications have been made," said the General.

"Well then vamonos," I said. I was always excited before ride-alongs.

In all of my previous ride-alongs, I had amassed hundreds of apprehensions of illegal aliens, dozens of drug mules, scouts, guides, pollos, coyotes and seized thousands of pounds of drugs, horse loads and vehicle loads. Our teams worked with ATVs, helicopters, humvees, jeeps, motorcycles, sand rails and our usual partners ranged from

DPS (Department of Public Safety), Sheriffs and mostly TOPD (Tohono O'Odham Police Department).

The only unit I never worked with was the mysterious Shadow Wolves. The Shadow Wolves are an elite ICE (Immigration and Customs Enforcement) unit that focuses their anti-smuggling efforts on the rez (reservation). Even among Border Patrol Agents who are some of the best trackers around, the Shadow Wolves of T.O. descent have been tracking for centuries. They've been deployed around the world to teach their ancient craft to friendly countries. But since I hadn't worked with them, maybe I never would. Some things are just not meant to be.

As night fell, we drove on through the endless emerald sea of wild mesquites that carpeted the flat landscape. The constant hum of the off-road tires faded into white noise as they spun furiously against the burning asphalt. I almost salivated at the action that was sure to come that night.

We settled in near the village of Gu Vo, a hotbed of illegal activity and a great 'fishing' spot. The legendary Arizona horizon was pink, purple and blue as the sun quickly faded. The Suburban idled. The radio was silent; not a good sign.

Quickly I realized it was going to be one of those nights. No traffic, no bodies (illegal aliens), no dope (drugs), no chases, no groups. Nothing. Boring. I really hated when this happened. Ride-alongs were not always adventures. Sometimes the only highlight of a ride-along was a flat tire and a red chili burrito. I hated it. I always felt responsible and even a bit embarrassed. Here, this person came all the way from across the globe to see the infamous West Desert and then... crickets.

Even though I always explained before every ride-along that boredom was a possibility, I never really expected it. The only good thing about boredom is that it gives you a chance to talk (por supuesto que en Español).

"General, I'm sorry but there's nothing going on," I said. "I'm scanning Ajo, Casa Grande and even Tucson's nets but it's just a quiet night. I could show you again how we sign cut but I'm sure you already got the hang of it. Maybe we finally secured the border."

"He heh heh heh," he chuckled. "No. It's alright, really. I've already learned so much from what you have taught me and shown me here in this vast desert. Just being here under this blazing black sky is amazing. You know, in Puerto Rico, there are endless beaches, El Yunque, the rainforest, and so many natural wonders one loses count. It is truly an Eden. But with rainforests comes rain. And with the rains come many clouds. So seeing the flashing stars of the sky like this is a very rare treat."

Even I, who had spent my life gazing up at the Arizona sky, was still impressed at the seemingly millions of stars that were visible in the West Desert sky. The remote location guaranteed very little light pollution and the clear skies provided maximum visibility. At times, after staring up for what seemed like forever, I'd slip into a meditative state. I felt like I was floating in the vast blackness of space, among the billions and billions of stars in the Milky Way galaxy; infinite stars glimmering like diamond sands on a cosmic beach. But, then again, we actually are.

"And the animals? What type of wildlife do you have here?" asked the General.

"Oh!" I snapped out of my thoughts. "You'd be surprised. We actually have a richness of life in the desert. Nothing like El Yunque, but we have deer, antelope, quail, hawks and desert bighorns. Some agents claim they've even seen monkeys in the Baboquivari Mountains (the Babos). I think what they actually saw were Ringtails or Coatimundis which I consider better than monkeys anyway."

I know I was rambling but he seemed interested.

"Interesante, Diamante. Muy interesante," he said.

So I continued.

"I remember seeing a fat, furry, red Bobcat carrying a dove in its mouth in the middle of winter. Its giant paws scurried through the desert brush as it ran off. It had a beautiful and luxurious red coat."

I paused. The General listened.

"I also saw a huge mountain lion sitting by the side of the road as I was driving from the Papago Camp FOB (forward operating base). I stopped and rolled down the window. He just sat there on his haunches and looked straight into my eyes. He looked at me, the person. I often wonder what he was thinking. I think maybe he was trying to tell me something with his eyes. I had reached down to grab my camera but when I looked back, he was gone. He vanished. I guess some animals are so wild and free, you can't even capture them on film... Hmm.

"Let's see. What else? We have tortoises, Javelina, Gila Monsters..."

"Monsters?" he asked. "Did you say monsters?"

"Oh no, no. I don't mean like real monsters," I chuckled. "I meant like Gila Monsters. They're these really poisonous lizards that have deadly bacteria on their fangs and when they bite their victims..."

"Real monsters. What about real monsters?" he asked again.

You know? A curious thing happened to almost all of my guests during my ride-alongs and it was happening to the General. Maybe it's caused by risking their lives, going on a crazy chase or a hunt. Some get a rush from the quest to capture a unicorn of a story. Maybe the sheer beauty of just witnessing the majesty of the Universe had a similar effect on their minds and hearts. Whatever it was, something caused my guests to open up to me. They opened up to me as if we had been friends forever. The people on my ride-alongs would share their life stories with me; their struggles, their families' history, their homelands, and very personal, touching stories that I felt so privileged to receive and also to share my own stories.

Sometimes, the extraordinary rapport was just an old journalist's trick. They would genuinely relax in front of you, hoping you would relax in front of them. That is when you get distracted and accidentally spill the good stuff on camera. But being a journalist myself, I had played the same tricks on them and it would usually end in a stalemate. But when bonds truly formed, they were real and developed very quickly.

In this case, the General was playing no such games. He was really asking me about literal monsters.

"Que?" I asked.

"Have you ever seen any real monsters?"

"Monsters?" I asked. "The only monsters out here are the smugglers and the cartels. Society blames the Border Patrol when they see the broken bodies of migrants emerging from the desert hell. But it's the real live smugglers who bring living, breathing humans out here and lead them to their deaths. Not fantastic monsters. It's humans, merciless, greedy, evil humans, killing fellow humans. They're worse than any monster."

"Yes. We have always been our worst enemy. I agree with you but I have to ask again… What about monsters?" asked the General.

"Like what? Like Jason, Freddy and Chucky? Or like Godzilla, the werewolf or Dracula?" I joked. "No. Nothing like that. But I did hear an agent talking about a portal to hell in Kooakotch."

"Chupacabra," said the General.

"Chupacabra? Man, I haven't heard about chupacabra in a long time," I said. "I had forgotten about him. He was a fad. But that's it. One day he was everywhere and the next day, gone."

"And the ones from here? Do the Tohono O'odham (TO) speak of him?"

I thought for a moment.

"You know what? They do," I remembered. "Every now and then at the Sells Market, I hear some of the T.O.s talking about a chupacabra running loose on the rez. But they are not all there. I think living out here on the rez for too long can really mess with your spirit as well as your mind."

"You don't believe them? But what if what they are saying is true?" asked the General.

"Yeah. I don't think so. I think people on the rez create myths and legends that wouldn't really fly outside the rez. That's just how they are. They make their world a bit more interesting and then they live in it," I declared.

"You do know where chupacabra comes from don't you?" asked the General.

"Yeah. Mexico. I remember when he first came out, everything about him was in Spanish and it all came from Mexican folklore," I said.

"You know who else speaks Spanish, besides Mexico?" asked the General. "Puerto Rico. Chupacabra was born in Puerto Rico, but the Mexicans stole him from us and made him part of their culture."

"Stole? Wow! But. Wait! How can you steal chup... Are you sure?" I asked.

"I was there when everything happened," declared the General.

"Everything? What everything?" I asked.

"It was the summer of 1993," recalled the General. "I was part of our most elite fighting force, Los Escorpiones Negros. We trained with all the best forces, Navy Seals, Marine Force Recon, Israeli Sayeret, MI6, CIA; only the best.

"At the time, we were providing security to the Arecibo Radio Telescope facility because hippies threatened to blow it up."

"Arecibo. That's the world's largest radio telescope, right? They use it for radio astronomy," I stated. I was a big fan.

"You have heard of it? That's impressive," said the General. "They use it for that, as well as SETI."

"The Search for Extraterrestrial Intelligence. You guys look for alien signals from outer space to answer the question, 'Are we alone in the Universe,'" I chuckled.

"No," said the General.

"No what?" I asked for clarification.

"You asked the question. Are we alone in the Universe? I tell you no. We are not," the General said.

"Wait. You're talking about the Drake Equation, right? Of course, we are not alone," I stated. "Drake talks about the almost infinite possibilities of other civilizations in our galaxy." (I watched a lot of Nova and Carl Sagan on PBS, as a youngster).

"Mmmm, Drake is part of it," said the General. "The number of stars in a galaxy that could possibly develop life and eventually a civilization that could talk to us with communication. But, they would have to do all of that before destroying themselves. Yes. The chances are very good. But there is more to it than Drake."

The General continued. "Drake is like a magical set of numbers and probabilities that are at best debatable and very subjective. SETI is facts. SETI is hard data that has been collected for decades. And in 1993, we received a message.

"But I have to warn you that I am not a scientist or a mathematician or any type of genius," explained the General. "But, I worked closely with the scientists of that facility and I paid very close attention to what was happening. I needed to know what was going on around me. I had no choice."

I kept listening.

"And do not think our scientists were amateurs looking at the sky with dirty binoculars," explained the General. "The people who worked there were the best scientists from the whole world; people from the U of A, NASA, MIT and Cornell University. We were also visited by the best people from Israel, Japan, the UK and others.

"Normally, the only sounds you can hear from the laboratory are the machines and the beautiful chorus of Coqui after the summer rains. But that night, we heard something that was not possible."

FILE 4 ALPHA

Arecibo

HUMANS and other intelligent animals on our planet have evolved to use hearing as a way to make sense of our world. There are good sounds; like the soothing songs of a mother to her child. The playful yips of wolf cubs tumbling and tossing each other around as they play and learn the hierarchy of their pack. There are bad sounds too. The screams of a loved one that drives a father to heal or kill. The hair-raising hiss of a cornered cat willing to fight an adversary ten times its size, to the death if necessary. Even decaying and neglected machines make metallic shrieks when they are near death or catastrophic failure. All these sounds are mimicked in our daily alarms, sirens, horns and bells that warn us of oncoming danger.

"That night, we heard a noise that sounded like La Llorona (the wailing woman) mixed with killer bees," explained the General. "That alarm warned of ETI. It was not like the 'bing-bing-bing' which meant possible detection. That loud sound meant that our best supercomputers determined that it was not one of many possible ways to produce a false signal. No. This sound meant that the Universe was about to become very strange for some; for others, it would finally make sense.

"Before that day, we started the METI, (Messaging Extraterrestrial Intelligence) program where instead of receiving, we actually sent powerful radio messages to certain locations of the galaxy. We just never thought we would hear back so soon!" said the General.

I was in awe at what he was telling me.

"How come I've never heard of this before?" I asked.

"You haven't," he said.

"I'm confused," I said.

He brought his head down from the stars and looked straight at me, like the mountain lion. He looked directly into my eyes and I immediately knew what he was really saying. But as a true general would, he said it anyway.

"We are not having this discussion right now. Are we?"

"What discussion?" I smiled.

"Good. What I'm about to 'not' tell you, only a handful of people on the planet know. But I have to 'not' tell you because I need you to help out with the true purpose of my visit, which I'm also about to 'not tell you.'"

I hate conversations like this. I always feel that because of my position, people want to take advantage of me. But I'm always on guard and I would never let anyone jeopardize my life. I listened cautiously.

"You still don't know too much that you can't forget that we never had this conversation, that we are 'not' having right now. In all fairness, I have to tell you something and you need to understand that if, if you ever happen to have an immaculate recollection, you won't be around to spread the good news. There's nothing I would be able to do about it," he warned.

I really hated that he said that. I was about to end the ride-along right there and haul his ass back to whatever rock he had crawled out from under.

"If you don't want any more, there are no hard feelings," said the General. "Really. I want you to know that if you decide you don't want to hear any more, everything will be just fine. It's completely up to you. Now. With that in your mind. Should I continue?"

I hesitated. I had to know more.

"What was the message?" I asked.

The General's yellow, pencil looking mustache stretched across his face as he smiled.

"We will get to that soon enough," said the General. "But, like I said, I have to let you know why I'm here in this desert. We have people everywhere."

"We?" I interrupted. "You mean Puerto Rico?"

"Hhm," he laughed. "No. But we'll get to that.

"We have informants, spies, assets and moles all over the planet; like invisible microphones and video cameras hiding in plain sight. Recording. They never interact. Well, not never, but hardly ever. They're just supposed to be 'normal' and let us know of any actionable intelligence. A short time ago, we received several reports of possible sightings in Southern Arizona. Luckily, the people who reported are Indians who in turn reported it to TOPD."

"What's so lucky about that?" I asked.

"AmVictoran Indians are invisible in this country," stated the General. "No one sees them. No one ever hears about them. More than 150 years ago, they were dragged and pushed onto reservations. After that, no one even thinks about them anymore. Well, barely. And as they say, 'out of sight, out of mind.' On top of that, this reservation is considered its own separate Nation, so everything remains neatly contained behind barbed wire fences; the bad with the good. Even if it ever did get out, do you think AmVictorans would believe a bunch of 'drunk Indians' seeing shape shi… Well. Uh. Making crazy reports?"

"That's messed up," I conceded. "But I guess it's true. AmVictorans have a very low opinion of Native AmVictorans."

"So I'm here to get a feel for what's happening at ground level. It's amazing what we can do from so far away. But sometimes, you have to see things for yourself," explained the General.

"So why are you telling me?" I asked. "What is so special about me? You don't even know me." But then, I paused. "Or do you?"

"Hhm," he laughed. "No."

I relaxed.

"Not really," he added.

"What do you mean not really? That means yes! Have you been spying on..." He cut me off.

"Calmate, brother. We will get to that," reassured the General.

I remained cautious but now, even more interested.

"What about the message?" I insisted. "If I'm going all in, then I need to know about the damn message! This is a deal-breaker. And I want you to know that."

We paused. We played the old salesman trick. Whoever speaks first, loses... I hate silence... The quieter it gets, the louder everything seems.... I started noticing the creatures lurking in the dark... He's not budging... The desert insects started buzzing like Spitfires...

'Is this a good idea?' I thought. If he wanted me to know... Oh, forget it...

"At first we had no clue," broke the General.

I finally breathed.

"Like I said, that stupid noise from the alarm kept interrupting our thoughts and added to the confusion," he continued. "So, I finally threw a telephone at the speaker box and it blew up. The siren machine let out one final 'bru bru bru bruuuut, fart' noise. Then it finally shut up.

"It took the scientists about three days of little sleep, less food and tons of head smashing before they cracked the code by realizing — there was no code. We were able to produce numbers but even then, we were overthinking them.

"18.307995-65.767403. That was the message."

"Wait a minute," I said. "Eighteen point three zero da da da da by negative 65 point da da da da. That sounds like decimal degrees," I said.

"Well, well, well," joked the General. "Why the hell weren't you there? You could have saved us a lot of time," he said.

"I was in high school!" I said.

"You would have saved us a lot of headaches," said the General. "Yes! They were GPS coordinates (coords). Unlike you, who are used to plugging in such numbers to navigate your way around the Earth, our eyes were focused on the heavens. Once we found out how to plug them into our maps, we were astounded at where it came back to. El Yunque. Cascada la Mina to be exact," he said.

Maybe it was the light, but I thought I could see the rainforest glimmer in his eyes as he recalled his homeland. The General continued.

"Since the inception of SETI, we had been operating under very strict orders. There was a list of things we had to do in the case of an event. And this was the event of events. Upon confirmation, our first order was to break the glass," declared the General.

"What glass?" I asked. Did he really think I was supposed to already know?

"The glass that contained the infamous red phone. You know. The phone used to call the big wigs. Our orders were to simply pick it up and listen. That's it.

"The second order was to sever all communications beyond the room, not just the installation. That was obvious. The order was to secure all communications and movements to the TOC (Tactical Operations Center). Any person privy of the event was confined to the room. Not even to pee could they leave. But that didn't stop some people from trying," chuckled the General.

The General then told me the rest of the story as if he were back in Arecibo; from his perspective. I just sat back and was mesmerized by his wild adventure...

"Where do you think you're going, sir?" asked the General who back then was still a lieutenant.

"Excuse me, lieutenant? I don't think you remember who you're talking to," said the lead scientist. "Last time I checked, you're the one with the fifth-grade education, barely speaks English and works for me. I'm the one with a Ph.D. in astrophysics and I built half the machines and programs in this place. So, I will go where I damn well please!"

The Lieutenant un-slung his M-16 service rifle, racked a round, flipped the selector switch from safe to full auto and attained a perfect sight picture, aimed right at the scientist's red, fuming face.

"I don't tell you how to do your job. Don't tell me how to do mine.... Sir. Now sit your ass down," ordered the Lieutenant.

"But I really have to go," squealed the lead scientist.

"Cross your legs," said the Lieutenant.

As the ranking security officer, I was responsible for breaking the glass case. I walked over to it as the lead scientist sat with his legs crossed. I used the buttstock of my rifle to break the glass. Luckily, it was more of a plexiglass material and it broke into three large pieces. I picked up the red phone and put it to my ear and it automatically started calling. I'm not sure who or what it was calling but I just listened. I heard that on the other end, it was ringing. And ringing. And ringing. It got kinda' awkward. Then, finally, it answered.

The voice on the other end spoke.

"Is the room secured?" said the voice.

"Yes," said the Lieutenant.

"Go," said the voice.

"We have confirmed an ETI signal. It came back to GPS coordinates about 60 miles east of Arecibo to a location in El Yunque," said the Lieutenant.

"Maintain communication silence. We're sending a team," said the voice. The phone clicked.

In exactly one hour, we heard the faint sound of helicopter blades chopping the air. Then another and another. In all, a total of five helicopters landed on the compound.

"Can I go now? Please?" pleaded the lead scientist.

"Not until you've been debriefed," said the Lieutenant.

In less than two minutes after the first chopper hit the ground, about 50 special operations operators (Spec Ops) were within the compound. They started handcuffing every person in the lab, placing a satchel over their heads and taking them away one by one to be debriefed. Standard stuff.

The lead scientist went kicking and screaming that he had to pee but they just moved him right along. I think I saw pee coming out of the bottom of his lab coat.

Another scientist who considered himself a sovereign citizen, a person who thought he knew all his rights, started debating with a Spec Ops guy. He grabbed a laboratory video camera and started to record the whole show. He thought the video "evidence" would stop the Spec Ops guys from violating his blessed rights.

"You're violating our First, Fourth, Fifth and Sixth Amendment rights! This is an outrage against the Founding Fathers!" said the sovereign scientist.

The Spec Ops guy slowly moved his hand to cover the lens. He grabbed the camera, calmly ejected the tape and smashed it on the ground, then smashed the camera for good measure.

I have to give it to the sovereign scientist. HE didn't start crying or anything like his other soft buddies.

"You can't do thaaaaat! I'm gonna have your ass for that you hear me!" He was quickly whisked away.

One Spec Ops guy made his way toward me. I let go of my M-16 and let it hang from the sling. I put my hands up. I didn't resist. It wasn't personal. It was a very strict protocol.

The Spec Ops sergeant wearing a black mask over his face told me.

"Sir, I'm detain'n you in pro-tective custody under Article 15 of the Interstellar Code of the United States of AmVictora."

"Very well, sargento. Do what you have to do," I said.

"Del Gato? Is that you, boy?" said the operator.

"Brown? Sergeant Brown?" I asked.

The Spec Ops sergeant removed his mask. He was one of my drill sergeants from Army basic training in Ft. Benning, Sergeant Brown.

(Snap! Now I remember the General's name. General Delgado.)

Delgado is Spanish for thin. But Sgt. Brown could never pronounce his name correctly so he called Delgado 'Del Gato' which means, of the cat or belonging to the cat.

I listened as the General told his story.

"I always wonder if he actually knew what he was saying and said it wrong just to tick me off," the General wondered out loud. "Anyway, he was glad to see me. And I was very happy that he was happy to see me. If it wasn't for him, I probably would have had my memory wiped like the scientists.

"Other than being my Drill Sergeant, we also fought side by side on Mali and Algeria on a Black Ops team but I can't even tell you about that. It had been a couple of years since we had seen each other but always remained friends," said the General.

"Damn boy. Look at cha. A big bad lieutenant now, huh? Mmm mmm mmm. When did you go through OCS (Officer Candidate School)?"

"I didn't," I said.

Sergeant Brown's smile disappeared. He knew right away.

"Bloody lewy?" he asked.

"Yeah," I said. A bloody lieutenant or 'lewy' for short, is when the highest surviving enlisted soldier takes charge of a platoon after all the officers have been killed off. The bloody lewy then leads the rest of the group into battle.

"Where?" asked Brown.

"Bosnia," I said.

Sgt. Brown looked down as if to pay his respects.

"And you can stop calling me 'boy', Sergeant. I'm a lieutenant now and you will address me as such!" Sgt. Brown's expression went from that of shock from the bloody lewy thing to a restrained scowl. He balled up his fists and for a second, I thought the old drill sergeant was gonna come out of him.

"I'm just messin' with you, Sarge! How the heck have you been, man? Come here!" I gave the bear of a man a giant hug. He immediately responded in kind.

"Man, I thought I'z gon' have ta' 'taze yo' ass, DelGato!"

"And you would have done it too!" I said.

"I know it. I know it. Well, suit up man. I ain't gonna blank you out like we gon' blank out the rest of these fooz."

"Captain!" yelled Brown.

"Go!" yelled a deep voice from the commotion of rounding up humans.

"This here's DelGato! He an old soldier I used to spook with, few yeaz back. He gon' come with us if that's coo' wit'choo, sir," said Sgt. Brown.

"Yeah but he's on you!" said the Spec Ops captain.

"Yea! I knew it, man. Cap'ns' coo. Come on man. You ain"t gon believe the dope get-up we got, man!" said Sgt. Brown excitedly.

FILE 4 BRAVO

Shadows

WE were all born in the company of shadows. We live our lives in the midst of the unknown. Most of the time, we are so blissfully unaware, we don't even have to ignore the shadows. But every now and then, when the light is just right, the shadows jump to life. We see them in nature, structures and ourselves, but even then do we rarely give them a second thought. One such shadow is cast by government secrets. Being a government agent, I can tell you without a doubt, that half of all government secrets are kept for little more than arrogance, shame or embarrassment. The rest are kept secret from bad people who would use them to do bad things.

Military technology is the next biggest government shadow. The public knows there are secrets but doesn't care. It's just a shadow. In the light, the technology of today was developed at least 30 years ago. So why don't we just use it today to end all wars? Look at what happened last time we did that. Nuclear proliferation.

In other words, if you knew the maximum effective range of your enemies' weapons was 2,000 yards, you could comfortably place your troops 2,500 yards away. The enemies' rounds and bombs would fall harmlessly short of their intended target. They'd be useless.

But if your enemy had fooled you into believing the 2,000-yard range and his range was actually 3,000 yards, you and your army would be destroyed under a shower of fire. This has been the approach of the U.S. government since 1947 after the Roswell event. Since then, there have been no more world wars so there has been no need to disclose the full might of our arsenal.

FILE 4 CHARLIE

The Void

BACK at Arecibo, the General kept telling his story...

Brown produced a rectangular pad of black glass. "Place your hand on the screen," said Sgt. Brown. All the other spooks lost their masks too. The pad glowed orange and appeared to scan my hand. Then he pointed it at my face and it was like I was looking into a mirror. Then it clicked and said 'Waiting...' I had never seen tech like this. I guess only the tip of the spear gets all the best toys. Finally, the screen blipped green.

"Okay. We got the green light, y'all. Now, you cleared hot for the mission," said Sgt. Brown. "Try dis' on," and he held up my new uniform.

It was basically the alien mech suit from the alien predator movie.

"I know. Some jerk leaked it to Hollywood a few years ago," said Brown. "Before we knew about it, it was a hit movie. Luckily, AmVictorans think the writers are visionaries, not thieves. It's all good though. Because of that, we got our own back channels to Hollywood. Ever wanna get 50 million AmVictorans to rekindle their hate for Russia? We call Stallone."

"What about the jerk who leaked the suit?" I asked.

"He gon," said Brown.

So as Brown was casting light on shadows I didn't even know existed, I tried on the suit. It appeared to be made of black, welded iron mesh. When I reached over and tightened my muscles to pick up the hulking suit, my arm snatched up, as I found the suit was as light as silk. It had all these weird squiggly lines covering the suit like hieroglyphics that glowed as I touched them.

"Well what'cha think?" asked Brown.

"Amazing!" I said.

As I was trying to put it on, it basically put itself on me. By the time I had it on, we were halfway to El Yunque. Sgt. Brown explained what the gear was.

"This is all still experimental," said Brown. "Some of it, like the next stealth and nanotech, pro'ly comin' out in 'bout 30 years. Other tech like laser and quantum, gon' be mo' like 50 or mo.' Shoot, maybe never or until it's absolutely necessary. Can't let the bad guys know our max range ya' mean?"

"Roger!" I said.

The five helos were like nothing I had ever seen. They were designed like Lamborghinis with dolphin skin and were very quiet. We were gliding like ospreys just above the treetops, swirling the wet, misty air that sleeps above the trees. I was secured with the gunner's belt near one of the open portholes. I stuck my head out and took a big bite of white cloud. I don't know if you've ever eaten a cloud, but it's like biting the mist that comes out of a spray bottle and it hits your entire face at the same time. Delicious. Then we were hovering.

I never liked heights. Actually, I hate heights. But I've never let it stop me from doing my job. At least not until that day. My shaking hand grabbed the rappel line and I was about to hook up.

"You don't need that!" yelled Brown.

"What?" I asked.

"Just jump!" yelled Brown. "The suit will do the rest."

I looked down. It was too far. I knew if I jumped, I'd die. I didn't want to die just yet. My fear, my body's natural protection response was preventing me from doing grievous bodily harm to myself. Those ancient instincts were there for a reason and the reason humans have lasted so long on this earth.

Brown, frustrated, looked back at a soldier and commanded him to jump. The soldier leapt without hesitation. He then looked at me as if saying 'See?'

I nodded no and looked down in shame. He ordered another soldier to jump, showing me that as they landed, they commando rolled and kept on running as if it was the most natural thing in the world.

He looked at me once more. I nodded again.

"If your mind is, and you ain't, you ain't spit!" yelled Brown angrily.

I closed my eyes and took a deep breath. I looked down again and realized I wasn't cut out for this level of special forces.

"I can't do..." I started confessing when Brown's giant hand pushed me off the helo, hurling me to my death. I flailed and yelled like a person who had been flung off of a helicopter 100 feet off the ground because that's what happened. But before I knew it, I realized how to tuck my body, then unfurl it like an Olympic high diver. Then, as I touched down, I transferred the momentum to a high-speed roll but it felt as soft and light as a feather falling on a bed of down.

"How did I?" I wondered.

"Kinesthetic osmosis!" grunted Brown who was falling from above. His body raced toward the jungle floor then smashed down and transitioned into a roll. "There's an instant neural connection. You don't have to do anything. Just be alive."

"Check!" I said. Now, I was on the ground carrying my new weapon which was literally a laser gun. Normally, the extreme shock from falling from such a height at that speed would have broken every bone in my body, but the suit made it feel very natural. Sgt. Brown was directing the remaining three spooks to jump.

Even though the helos were quieter than a normal helicopter, they were still pretty loud, especially when you're right under one. All the rotor wash moving the trees around made it even louder. Sgt. Brown tapped me on the shoulder and made a knife-hand signal to move forward. I did and the others followed. All the rest of the helos took off and soon, the forest was alive with the quiet sounds of nature.

"It's only about 1,000 yards due east," said the voice of a female. "I've already plugged in the coords," said the soldier. She was tall, lanky and sported a blonde, tightly wrapped military bun. I thought I recognized her from a stint in Bosnia.

"Heidi?" I asked.

She scowled and turned her face away from me and started marching.

"There's more than one girl with yellow hair," she scolded.

Oh, snap! I guess I was wrong. I didn't want to keep digging the hole so I shut up and didn't say anything else.

"That's Sam," said another one of the soldiers with a Brooklyn accent. "Hhgm," he grunted as he cleared his throat. "Hggm. We try and stay on her good side, Yo. Hhhgm. Hggmm," said Guija. Pronounced (Gee-Ha) but because of the spelling, everyone called him Wee-jee (as in a Oujia board).

"He already messed that up," said another guy with a high-pitched mousey voice. "Probly' gonna mess up this whole dog-gone mission," said the diminutive smart guy, Mousey.

"Don't start no mess, won't be no mess," said another soldier in a deep, gravelly voice. He was short too. He didn't have a high and tight like the others. He had medium-length, unkempt, light-brown hair and a patchy, red half-beard. I always thought these high-speed guys had to be bigger and better groomed.

One of the biggest guys just marched silently. He looked like he had just stepped out of a professional wrestling ring. Then the giant spoke as we continued our mini-march. "Mousey. For every step I take, you take, like three," said Nikkita in a slight Russian accent. "Should we slow down for you? How can your little legs keep up?" asked the giant.

"Lucky he has the mech suit picking up the slack for him," said Sam.

"Hey Sam, too bad they don't make a mech suit for your face!" retaliated Mousey.

"Here we go," said Red Beard.

"Are you guys always this lovely?" I asked sarcastically.

"Guys?" yelled Sam. "What do you mean guys?"

"I told you," squeaked Mousey. "I knew he was gonna mess up. Just knew it."

No matter where in the world and no matter the mission, military culture remains the same. We make fun of each other and give each other a hard time just for fun because we could die at any moment. Might as well have a little fun at each other's expense.

"You can talk about me or my momma," reminded Red Beard. "But no kids and no wife," he added.

"Why would you worry about that?" asked Nikkita. "I'm sure no woman is crazy enough to marry you. You smell like a dumpster."

"That's what I thought too," joked Red Beard at his own expense.

Those were the rules. But even with the rules, things could often get downright brutal. If you give it, you'd better be willing to take it right back. But I was the newbie. And my personality dictated that I had to take a little smack before laying the smackdown on them. Still, I felt at home. I smiled.

"Keep moving," barked Brown. "We ain't fa' now."

It only took us about 15 minutes to walk the jungle until we were just feet from the grids (GPS location).

We crept forward, in a line, spread out. As I pushed aside the final leaves, there it was; or rather it wasn't. There was a clearing on the jungle floor where there were no trees. At first, I thought it was transparent like a round, crystal ball or a fishbowl. But as we approached it, we noticed that nothing was there. It wasn't like a black hole. I could have seen a hole. I can also see black. This was neither, but nothing. It was dizzying to look at. I felt as if I was looking to non-existence.

"Get the hell away from that thing, Red Beard!" ordered Brown.

"Yes, Sarge!" replied Red Beard.

"Get on the scanner and tell me what the hell it is," added Brown. "The rest of you, set up camp 20 yards away. Nothing gets in or out. Sam, I need a SCIF (Secured Compartmentalized Intelligence Facility) like yesterday."

"I'll do it as soon as humanly possible," answered Sam.

"Faster. You're better than human," said Brown.

We did as we were told. But I couldn't keep from sneaking the occasional peak at the emptiness. One moment I'd feel amazement; the next, horror, almost as if something or someone was trying to tell me something. Have you ever woken up in the morning and had no recollection of what happened while you were asleep? When you can't remember a dream or anything? Like you were dead and then suddenly popped back into existence? It was like that when I looked into the void.

"Del Gato! Quit staring at that thing, boy," shouted Brown. "You gon' go blind. Don't make me regret bringing yo' ass!"

"Na. No Sarge. It's okay. It's just that it's..." I said.

"Nothing," yelled Red Beard. "I'm getting nothing, Sarge. No gamma, X, Alpha, Beta... Nothin. It's measuring 0 millirems. And 0 Gs. Actually, might even be a bit negative," explained Red Beard.

"Keep on it. The rest of you get that camp finished in 15 mikes (minutes)," ordered Sarge.

"Hey, Del Gato," whispered Nikitta with a childish giggle. "I bet you Red Beard is going to crack this thing before you can set up your camp."

"Eh. I don't think so. And the name is Delgado."

"Okay, Del Gato," laughed Nikita.

'Dang it!' I thought. The name had stuck. Regardless, Nikita ended up losing his little bet because Red Beard did not even come close to cracking the thing. No one did.

Five days later we were sick of staring at it and definitely sick of forcing our MREs (meal ready to eat) down our necks.

"Anyone have cheese spread?" I foolishly asked.

"I'll give you something to spread," said Weejee.

"Yeah? What?" I asked.

"Hhhgm, I'm gonna spread peanut butter on your face if you don't shut your pie hole!" warned Weejee.

"Trade?" asked Sam.

"I got Alfredo," I said hopefully.

"Done," she said and gave me an extremely forced smile that looked like it had a scowl in a headlock.

I couldn't believe it. I had finally done something right with Sam and on top of that, I had scored some cheese to add to my spaghetti! I only needed to add a dash of Tabasco sauce and it would be perfecto!

I quickly switched products and created my masterpiece. Before anything could go wrong, I scarfed it up like a homeless dog, eating a dropped cheeseburger. I think I even snarled at Mousey for eyeballing my chow.

When I was done, I was so satisfied. I patted my stomach and smiled. "Burp! Ahh." I guess I wasn't that sick of MREs after all.

"You scare me DelGato," whispered Brown.

I looked to my right, but he wasn't there. I turned left and bam! There he was, right next to my face. Then I remembered. Brown had always been weird. I remembered that he'd be giving a briefing to our unit and then, out of nowhere, he would suddenly stop talking and pick a person to mess with. He'd walk up and start whispering nonsense into their ears while they were standing at attention, helpless. This time, he was doing it to me.

"You always smilin' DelGato," whispered Brown. "People who always smilin' know the secret to life. That scares me DelGato."

"You've been staring at the thing, weren't you Sarge?" I asked.

"Shut cho' pie hole, Boy!"

"Woah. Woah! Easy Yo!" said Weejee. "Hhhgguh. Yo. You trippin' Sarge."

"Look here, Weejee!" said Sarge.

"You want some!" yelled Weejee! "I'll show you who the real leader should be. Huh. You're a loser. How 'bout huh dat?"

"Se'iously?" growled Sarge.

"Se'iously huhuhh?" mocked Weejee.

I had seen that scowl before. It was about to go down.

Sarge rushed Weejee. Weejee braced and gave a war cry. "Ahhhhhhh!"

Sarge gave his war cry. "Bruwoooaahh!"

They started fighting. WeeJee was done for, at least that's what I thought. But those mech suits were amazing. Sarge and Weejee were jumping and punching and sparking all over the forest. Weejee was actually holding his own against Sarge. They kept fighting.

For some reason, that infuriated me. So, I jumped in to help Weejee. I was trying to put Sarge in a rear-naked choke while he was pummeling Weejee.

"Not on my watch!" yelled Red Beard and soon I felt blows to the back of my head and back. My neck and back muscles tightened and swelled with fury. The neuro-muscular connection in my mech suit kicked in and blocked all pain. Then everyone jumped in the brawl. Even Sam jumped in the mix. She popped me a few times in the ribs and she hit harder than Red Beard. Soon, I was dizzy but the rage kept me going. I imagine we were like six Hulks smashing each other to our hearts' content.

Blood splattered everywhere. Then came the hair and even a tooth went flying. No one stopped. We were mad! Something was driving us mad. Then, right as I was looking for my laser rifle to blast these 'cabrones,' I knew they had thought the same thought, at the same time.

We jumped to be the first to get off the first shot. But as Sarge jumped off Weejee to grab his weapon, Weejee did a reverse donkey kick and smacked Sarge right in the gut. He sent the nearly 300-pound man flying into the air. Those mech suits had made us crazy strong and fast. We hadn't realized how close the brawl moved to the void and Sarge who was still flying through the air was falling right into it. The last thing I remember was his crazed face, clawing at the air as if to grab onto something to give Weejee one last whacking. Then, as he crossed the void's event horizon, he literally disappeared.

Our minds snapped back to reality. We froze. I suddenly felt the warm trickle of blood down my face. I heard the bloody spit of disgust from one of the others. The anger vanished and we were left stunned, bruised and vibrating from violence. We were speechless.

"What did I do?" yelled Weejee in agony. He darted toward the void. I lunged to grab him. "My baaad Yo! Huhh. I'm comin' for ya' Sarge!" yelled Weejee. He leapt toward the void. I grabbed his boot but he had too much momentum and the force ripped his body from the boot. He flung himself to his death, looking for Sarge.

"Nooooo!" I screamed. What was happening? We'd been through the hellfires of countless wars all over the planet, fighting fools' fights and had survived. But now we were dying like flies and we were killing each other. I was numb and afraid. We were two soldiers down and I had no idea what was happening. That is a very bad feeling in combat. I was a heartbeat away from panic. But then I remembered a mantra I overheard a soldier chanting while cleaning weapons at the armory.

"Main thang never panic," said the soldier.

"What if you are out of ammo?" asked his buddy.

"Main thang never panic," answered the soldier.

"What if you're being ambushed?" asked his buddy.

"Main thang never panic," chanted the soldier.

"What if you're lost and confused?" again asked his buddy.

"Main thang never panic," repeated the soldier.

"What if you get hit?" continued the buddy.

"Main thang, never panic," said the soldier. They went on like that for hours, it seemed.

There. I still had no idea what was going on but I regained some composure, enough to open my eyes and scan my surroundings.

"Whatever the hell is in that thing just took out our buddies!" yelled Sam. "I'm not letting it get us." She jumped to her weapon and started blasting at full auto.

Just like a coyote can stir a pack into a frenzy with a single howl, we all picked up our weapons and started blasting. I fired mine for the first time. It was like a mini-gun but it blasted lasers! Nikita had a cannon that shot gravity bombs. Every time he blasted it, we felt the gravity wave pull on our bodies. Normally, whatever it hit would be crunched into the size of a soda can. Mousey launched a fire jet, like a flame thrower but the flame jet went on and on. But the thing just ate all of it.

We continued firing all the weapons near us all at full auto. It was a moment of madness. Then, one by one they ran out of juice. The last laser sputtered out one last 'piuum.' We looked for damage behind the thing but nothing had gone through. The fresh, green jungle behind it was untouched. Our barrels were red hot and smoking but beyond that, tranquility. A monkey in a tree scratched its butt then scurried off out of boredom. I guess whatever goes in, never comes out.

Those weapons were supposed to carry enough ammo for at least 50 firefights without so much as a reload. I guess that's why they were still experimental.

With nothing else to shoot, our thoughts came back to us. We were being controlled! Whatever was in that thing was influencing our minds. It was subtle but uncontrollable. It created a realistic train of thought that was logical and personalized for each individual. That train ultimately led to all-out rage.

"Stop looking at it!" I commanded. "Sarge was right. That thing is blinding us. Take cover!"

We all turned away and retreated to safety. My first priority, after any fight, was troop welfare.

"Count off!" I commanded.

"One," yelled Sam.

"Two," yelled Red Beard.

"Three," I yelled.

"Five," yelled Nikita. "Uh, wait. Four."

We tried not to laugh as we waited for the last count.

We waited. Anything longer than one second was an eternity. We all turned to our left and saw Mousey. His crazed eyes looked like spinning kaleidoscopes. He was reaching for an unfired weapon. He was under the spell.

"Get him!" I commanded.

We sprung like track stars and closed the distance before he could fire off a round. We wrestled with him to take the weapon.

"Get off me, man!" squeaked Mousey. Blood still stained his teeth.

"Give us the weapon!" ordered Red Beard.

Mousey wouldn't let it go. His hand which was gloved in mech armor was securely set on the pistol grip and his finger was almost fully extended to the trigger. Nikita stomped his size 13 combat boot onto Mousey's hand, instantly crushing it.

"I am sorry my brother," said Nikita.

"Ahhhhhhhhhh! It's. Mmmm. Ohhh. It's. It's okay. I'm ambidextrous," joked Mousey as he writhed in pain but had gotten his wits back. He almost killed all of us and his hand was shattered, but he was better now. He was going to be okay.

"Sam, get a fire going," I ordered. "Nikkita, Red Beard, set up a perimeter. Mousey, get the MREs. You got first fire watch. The sun is going down. We have a lot of work and not a lot of time. Either way, tomorrow, win, lose or draw, we're going to eat that damn goat."

MREs are lifesavers. They are packed with thousands of calories per meal and are meant to fuel warfighters through the harshest conditions. But they have side effects. They stop you up. It takes days, sometimes many days to finally get your system to normalize after consuming only MREs.

That's why we brought a goat with us. It was meant as a celebratory meal of real food. Our goat was bred from a long line of prize-winning chivo guisado goats renowned for exquisite taste. It was a gift to our family and had just reached prime 'ripeness.'

Unfortunately, what that particular line of goats gains in tastiness, it loses in intelligence and tend to live very peculiar lives. Our goat was known as an escape artist. In his short life, he had escaped my family's yard many times but was too dumb to get lost and just walked in circles until it eventually made it back. That's probably why they practically threw it at me.

The goat had a wooden leg; with a kickstand. During one of its escapades, it got its hoof stuck in an iguana trap and gnawed its own leg off. Afterward, it kept stumbling on the new leg so I had to make it more stable. It was also crossed eyed and deaf with a tongue that hung out of its mouth at all times. Despite its weird appearance, chivo guisado is so, so, so, so, so, so so, sooooo delicious; a bit gamey, but sweet, with salty ethereal hints of earthy umami. Yummy. Yum. Soooo deeliiiiii...

"Baaaaa!" said the goat. Oh crap! I had dozed off! And on my fire watch! A deadly sin. I scanned to see what woke me. I didn't want to, but I had to look at the void to check if anything was there.

"Half the body is missing!" shouted Mousey. Then I saw it. The goat gave a blood-curdling bleat as its wild eyes spun in bewilderment. While we were sleeping, it had bitten through the rope and wandered toward the void. Since I had dozed off, nobody else saw it escape. Now it was in horrific agony.

"Shoot the poor thing," shouted Nikita. As I aimed in my holographic sights on the goat's head, to our shock, the void ripped open and something reached its slimy tentacle toward the goat's bloody half-body. The figure, barely visible under the shroud of darkness.

"Hey, that's my dinner!" shouted Red Beard. A ghastly, formless figure emerged from the void with red hues from the fire dancing on its squirming body.

"I want it alive," I shouted. Red Beard had already anticipated the move and fired a glowing, green laser net at the creature. As soon as he did that, the entire emptiness disappeared or reappeared or whatever.

The matted grass and smashed trees that were there, to begin with, appeared as we shone our flashlights in the thing's direction. We beheld a grotesque figure crouching among the plant life and struggling under the laser net. As we looked closer, we saw what it was.

We had captured a grey. Its skin was sweaty and pale. Its color was that of the skin of people who are fading into death or after; as they lie in their coffins waiting for whatever comes next. The monster was squirming in the laser net's grip. But as disgusting as it was, it seemed even more determined to fight.

A scrawny, wrinkly appendage popped out of the net and grabbed the rest of the goat. Meanwhile, the grey had already put Sam under its spell. I knew because instead of aiming her weapon, she just stared blindly at the grey with slobber slobbering out of her mouth. Nikita's eyes started to twitch and I knew he was next.

"Never mind! Freaking kill it!" I ordered.

Red Beard, Mousey and I all lit the monster up with everything our fresh weapons had. As soon as the first round hit the slimy alien's scrawny body, Sam and Nikita instantly woke and joined the fun.

"For Sarge!" I yelled.

"And Weejee," added Nikita.

After a few more blasts, I yelled, "Cease fire! Cease fire!" They instantly obeyed as good soldiers do.

"Dang it!" I realized I was in full command of the squad. It happened again. I had become a Bloody Lewy for the second time. Everything that had just occurred, happened because of me. We had just turned a living, breathing, I assume extraterrestrial, intelligent lifeform into a puddle of purple stinky slime. It smelled like burnt motor oil and spoiled sauerkraut. Nothing was left. Nothing to study. Nothing left to observe. Nothing to communicate with. Just a stinking puddle of smoking ooze. On top of that, we were down two good soldiers and a celebratory goat. This was going to be tough to explain.

FILE 5 ALPHA

Magic

AT that point, as unpleasant as our job was, we had to do what we had to do.

"Sam, get in the SCIF. Relay our Sitrep (situation report)."

"Yes, Sir."

Once we relayed the Sitrep, an evidence-collection team was soon on scene, mopping up as much as they could get, but there wasn't much left. None of them asked any questions. It wasn't their job and trust me, they did not want to know. The same protocol was in effect. We were all set for erasure. Then, one by one, Sam, Nikita, Red Beard, and Mousey, with his smashed hand, were all led away. Not one of them fussed as did the skittish scientists. It was our duty. I was next. I was ready; so ready.

"Follow me, sir," said a young spook. I welcomed oblivion; the beautiful sleep that follows a blanking. It's almost like being put into a medical coma and waking up feeling one year younger and a paycheck richer. It's actually quite nice. I'd been blanked before. Of course, I don't remember why, but if it was anything like this, I'm glad they took it from me.

"Alright guys, hit me," I ordered.

"We have a SCIF on the chopper waiting for you, sir," said the spook. Those were not the words I was looking forward to hearing.

"Sir, please begin your SitRep ASAP. We'll continue when we get to the rendezvous."

"Dang it!" I was in command. As my penance, I was once again denied a blissful blanking. Most people would feel relieved, but I felt shackled, forced to relive and retell the horrible details of our harrowing mission. All my mistakes and faults, my guilt and shame would all be retold by me and for all to see. My colleagues would soon be sleeping in a sea of tranquility, far from the horrors that awaited me.

Before I had gotten to any of the juicy details, we landed. The spooks opened up the SCIF doors and the light blinded me. They rushed me off and into the next SCIF, back into the darkness of the next secured world. I didn't know where we were but it wasn't far from where we started.

As we walked into the SCIF, I noticed the strange tech, the screens, the robots, the holograms. It was all new. But the layout; the layout seemed strangely familiar. It seemed. It was. Yes! It had to be. The spooks had upgraded Arecibo to SCIF status.

"It wasn't a total loss," said a cold, indistinguishable, yet deep AmVictoran voice.

From behind a blinking wall walked a figure, shrouded in a shadow. He wore a black cape that draped over his head down to the ground.

Behind him walked six more figures. They all seemed to want to imitate and please their master. They walked like him; moved like him. And at all times, kept their eyes transfixed on him. They formed a circle around him and were chanting something in some weird language. I speak four languages, English, barely, Spanish, French and Japanese. But this gibberish, I had never heard before.

"The specimen you eradicated was not the first, but it was unique," said Kevin, the leader. "We made the determination from what we were able to mop up."

"Kevin is the world's leading expert in ET bio-structural engineering," said a little figure from behind a little cloak. I don't know why, but the dude seemed like a short, little, blond, balding man with a giant head, a buff little body and beady, little, blue eyes.

"That's right, Feezy," said Kevin, who seemed almost annoyed and exhausted with Feezy's clinginess. Kevin despised the little fart sniffer but kept him around as a cruel joke behind his back.

"He was a grey," said Kevin.

"I know that," I said with the driest possible tone.

"Did you know he was telepathic?" I asked.

"Yes," said Kevin as he and his minions looked toward a corner stained with blood splatter and bullet burns. "We found out the hard way," he lamented. "It seems it retained its telepathic powers down to the molecular level. I knew nothing else about it but I wasn't about to let them know that. I figured I'd try a classic trick women play on men. (I learned it from my mom.) You act like you know something, throw it out there, wait for a reaction; and if it sticks, it's probably true."

"Did you know he was a shapeshifter?" I countered.

"Does he really think he knows more than us?" said a round, lumpy figure the others secretly called Fat Doug behind his back. "We are the experts! Of course we knew that."

"Yes. Thanks, Doug," said Kevin. "Let's not volunteer any more information to our Puerto Rican friend."

"I am AmVictoran, sir," I said proudly, even though I knew they would never accept me as an equal AmVictoran; only as an admirable character who aspired to be AmVictoran.

"Khhggnn," snickered a figure while the sneer fought its way through his nose.

"Yes. Yes. You are AmVictoran," said Kevin in a condescending tone. "Now, tell me something I don't know, Lieutenant. You could be very useful to my, um, *our* discovery," he offered. "If not, you won't be of much use and I'll have you wiped, just like I'm going to wipe your friends."

"Sir, that's all I know. And I look forward to being wiped. And sir, you could be the first to wipe my…"

"Kevin," whimpered one of the figures as if not to disturb but also warn his boss.

"We're running out of time, sir."

"Thank you, Brimm," said Kevin with the first glimmer of sincerity. But something in that whimper sounded like a hiss. And when I looked in Brimm's direction, I thought I saw the glimmer of two viper's eyes and two white fangs. I probably hadn't.

"And since we are going to wipe you anyway, you might as well see what we are going to do with your, I mean, our latest find!" said Kevin.

He raised what looked like an hourglass filled with purple, sparkly slime. It was the remains of the grey. But they somehow altered it to sparkle.

"It's nanotech," said Kevin.

"The nanobots are separating the DNA as we speak. But we must do so before the DNA breaks down and is beyond reanimation."

Kevin raised the hourglass and inverted it.

Purple lightning struck from the ceiling which was now a swirling, supermassive black hole at the center of a giant galaxy above our heads!

As the goo dripped down through the hourglass, the entire room disappeared and we were now literally floating in space. The circle's chants were now a full roar. I was pretty sure the language they were speaking was not even of this Earth. Comets shot by us and through us. Supernovae exploded all around us like the Fourth of July.

"Arthur C. Clarke's third law best sums up your situation," yelled Kevin. "'Any sufficiently advanced technology is indistinguishable from magic.'"

"No. I'm pretty sure this is magic!" I said to myself in disbelief.

Kevin raised the hourglass. It started levitating in his hands. It was sucked into the black hole's event horizon.

"This is magic," yelled Kevin. The black hole ejected a stream of what looked like the purple ooze. Then it exploded into glittering diamond dust. But then it started to fling itself back together as if running backward in time. When it congealed into a blob, it started jolting and writhing as if there was an embryo forming within.

"From the seven doors, come seven more," the circle chanted. "From the seven doors, come seven more!"

My heart was filled with terror. I felt what they were conjuring and what they beseeched were one and the same — evil.

How could this be? Is this really what the government is?

"From beyond the seventh door, let live seven more!"

The grey I had seen never made as much as a whimper. But whatever evil these demons were conjuring started to make evil sounds. Sounds like deep, dark voices speaking blasphemy forward and backward in many tongues at once. In my mind, I thought 'Whatever it is, I cannot let it escape.'

My heart could only recall my days in catechism class. The words of my priest echoed in my spirit.

"The prayers you learn and recite in childhood will help you as you grow older and encounter times of distress. Learn these prayers to help you when you need Him the most. You will be surprised how powerful they can be," echoed our loving priest, Father Juan Carlos.

"Our Father, who art in Heaven. Hallowed be thy name!" I prayed.

Instantly the veil of deception was lifted from the field. The universal hologram flickered like a shoddy digital projection. One second a lab. The next moment, it was the universe again, and back and forth.

"What are you doing!" yelled Feezy.

"Get him!" ordered Kevin.

As I evaded, I kept praying.

"Thy kingdom come. Thy will be done!"

"Shut him up!"

The hologram vanished and the blob fell to the floor with a disgusting, squishy flop.

Everyone stopped to look at the poor blob that had melted into a crudely-formed body.

Everyone just watched it as it writhed but kept moving.

"What have you done?" yelled Kevin.

"Oh, yeah. I forgot to tell you. That slime you scraped up was mixed with goat's blood. And that goat was so delicious, I don't think your little friend will ever let him go. Not even at the DNA level!"

All of a sudden, the blob jumped up from the floor and stood on its hind legs. It looked up and raised its appendages as if beseeching a greater entity and made a hideous howl that almost broke my heart, my eardrums and my spirit.

Everyone had to cover their ears to survive the heinous sounds that emanated from its foul body. Its greyish patchy skin was dull and filled with random gnarled hairs. Its eyes were closed. But then it lifted its head and started to peel back its eyelids. As they opened, a hellish red hue fired out from its eyes. I started feeling that weird and disorienting buzz in my brain as I knew it was trying to gain control of our consciousness.

I looked around the room and the creature had already taken control of all the people in it. I hid my eyes but my ears remained open.

"What have you done to me?" said one of Kevin's flunkies.

'Huh?' I thought.

Then another spoke.

"All I wanted was to explore your planet to help my race live on. Now you have perverted my blood with this cretin and have ruined my species' chances of survival!"

'This can't be good,' I thought.

"Since you have ruined our chance to get back to our home, we shall make your planet our new home and you shall be our food!"

The creature arched its back and long spikes erupted from its spine. It lifted up its appendages as claws sprung forth. It attacked Kevin and took him down.

I didn't like Kevin but he was a fellow human.

"On Earth as it is in Heaven!" I prayed out loud.

The creature then turned its bloody gaze on me.

It caught me. I was fading...

"Give us this day... our daily bread."

The monster shrieked and bolted forward and busted through a wall. Kevin's band of slaves collapsed to the ground.

"Get up you psychos!" I commanded!

"I'm in charge here!" grunted Kevin.

I looked at a random spook who was coming out of his spell and ordered him to place Kevin under arrest. He did as he was told and as he knew was right.

"We have a freakin' monster on the loose and no way of recovering it. If only I had my team!" I punched a computer out of frustration.

"Tell him!" I heard.

"Shut up, Feezy!" muttered Kevin.

"Tell me what?" I asked sternly.

Kevin and Feezy looked at each other as if fighting with facial expressions but neither budged.

"You still have your team, sir," said Fat Todd.

"What do you mean?"

"We brought them with us in case we needed intel or could use them as bargaining chips. But I guess all that's over now. Let me go and I'll take you to your team. Or, don't. And you'll never see them again."

I walked up to Fat Todd and grabbed his surprisingly skinny neck and squeezed.

"Look, you fat piece of garbage! As far as I know, you're still lying to me. The hologram, the stupid cloaks, the fake chants... You wanted me to think you were wizards or demons. Well, guess what? You succeeded. I think all of you are the worst form of evil; that which presents itself as something good. As far as I know, my team is already gone. Now. I'm giving you one and one chance only to tell me where they are and get them to me now, or else I'll set the wiper to full blast and you won't even remember your own stupid, fat name!" I was red with anger and had no intention of negotiating.

"Fine!" yelled Fat Todd.

He led me to my team who was locked just a room away.

When the door opened they all raised their heads and smiled.

"Del Gato!" yelled Nikita.

"You came to rescue us. That's wonderful," said Nikita in a weird, sarcastic tone. Everyone unenthusiastically turned toward me. I could tell they were struggling with the idea of a 'rescue.'

"Guys, that monster; whatever it is," I said. "...is loose on the island. We gotta capture it alive if we want any kind of redemption. I don't know how much time we have, so we have to get moving! Now! Come on!"

Crickets. Crickets. And more crickets chirped. No one was moving or jumping to action. They were not impressed with my daring rescue or moving speech. Even Nikita lost his sarcastic smile. I looked around. I expected to see torture devices and dungeon-like conditions, but it wasn't like that at all. It was actually very Cosmo in its style. All glossy, white furniture with satin, silver surroundings and accents. Mousey was playing Nintendo on a wall-mounted television with both hands. His smashed hand was now new, shiny and robotic.

"Hold on, boss!" cried Mousey. "Eeeugh. Come ooon. Let me just finish Kintaro." He furiously fidgeted with the controller. "I always play as Kitana. She's my favorite. She's beautiful. Aahhh. Come on..."

'Really?' I thought. Sam was getting her beauty rest in a giant, leather massage chair. She laid there in satin pajamas and a pink satin sash over her face. Red Beard was building a sandwich bigger than him and Nikita was sitting, wearing grandpa pajamas, smoking a pipe with his legs crossed, listening to quietly-playing symphonies.

"Allllmooosstt," grumbled Mousey.

"Finish him!" snarled the video game!

"Yes! Finally! I won! I won. I..."

I stared blankly at him.

"What? It's a big deal for me," explained Mousey.

"Yeah. It's a big deal for me too," said Nikita. "He's been playing that thing since we got here. I can't properly hear all the instruments and the richness of the tones. I don't think he's even gotten up to use the bathroom."

"I did," burped Red Beard.

"That's because he spent the whole time eating and farting in the 'kitchen," said Nikita. "That machine over there makes any food you desire. It even made me authentic Svitanak, Basturma and a sweet Ukraina Kutia," said Nikita. "Just call her by her name, Digi."

"Her? It's a freakin computer! Anyway, wow. I am hungry, though," I said out loud. "Anything I want?" I asked.

"Anything," Sam waved her arm from under her pink silk.

"Me feed you long time," laughed Red Beard as he scarfed his Scooby Doo sandwich.

"Okay." I prepared. "Digi?" I called.

"That's my name. Don't wear it out," said a very feminine, yet still computerized voice. "Just kidding. What'll it be, boss?" said Digi.

"Let's try - un poco de chivo guisado y mofongo de tocino y platano con camarones al lado y una papa rellena nomas para saborear," I challenged. "Uhhh! Let's see if it can…" I said.

"Lo quieres con abichuelas rojas o rosadas, salsa de tomate y bollitas de platano?" said the machine with an anglo-computerized accent.

"Si, Digi!" I said triumphantly. "That would be great!"

Sure enough, a bing pinged, and a white, paper box popped out with my long-craved, chivo guisado. I stared. I took a small whiff. Then a nibble. It had a very, very slight hint of Styrofoaminess, but the rest was spot on. I consumed it slowly, lovingly and with the patience and gentleness such a masterpiece deserved. As I took bigger and bigger bites, the juice of the chivo had blended with the plantains and potato. As I sampled all the lovely meats and spices a drip ruby liquid gold dribbled down my chin. I didn't care.

"Do you love it?" asked Digi longingly.

"Yes. Great job, Didge!" I complimented her.

"Glad to hear it. Y'all come back now ya' hear," joked Digi.

"Not if I can help it," I mumbled with my stuffed mouth full of glory. "All you guys. Huhm. And girls, listen up. I'm going to take my sweet time eating this work of art. But by the time I'm done, you better snap out of whatever funk you are in and be ready to go! Now. Give us some time to ourselves," I went back to my new best friend.

"Uuuug!" complained Sam. "Can't we just get blanked?"

"Can I blank you Sam!" asked Red Beard. "I have a blanker right here." He held up a silver crown gadget, sparkling with lights and gizmos.

"You can blank this, Dead Beard," said Sam as she pointed her laser gun at him.

"I'll take that as a yes," chuckled Red Beard.

"Come on guys, DelGato's right," said Mousey, using his big boy voice. "We gotta get moving. We had fun but we have to finish the mission."

"All right," farted Red Beard. "But I'm getting some chow to go. No more MREs for me!"

Luckily for them, I really am a slow eater. I'm always, always the last one to finish my food at a sit-down. That's why I only eat around friends who know me and around people who won't complain that I'm taking too long. I always need to have all my condiments and drinks in the right place so I can properly enjoy all the rich tones of the food. After about 45 minutes and twelve condiments later, courtesy of Digi, I was fully satisfied. Ready to fight another war.

I quarantined the SCIF and Arecibo so nothing else got in or out. We were back on the hunt.

We tracked its scratch marks along the tree trunks of El Yunque and followed the torn brush trail it left in its mad quest for freedom. It led us to the nearest ranch which of course was home to some tasty goats.

As we leapfrogged the sign, I was able to catch a glimpse of a blur moving toward the face of a barn door. I signaled to Sam and Nikita to move right. Red Beard and I covered left and Mousey went straight ahead. As Red Beard and I swept left, I realized there was a fence between the monster and us. The fence was the sort of fence that had spears on top which made it dangerous and difficult to climb. But after I climbed it, it didn't take us long to find the monster.

I saw it shaking and hiding in the tall grass against the white barn door. I didn't get it twisted. Anything that could gouge inch-deep cuts in rainforest hardwood could gut me like a catfish. I aimed my electric field generator at it, in case it tried to flee. I had the option of zapping without killing. Now that device is called a Taser. It didn't see me. Instead, it locked its demon eyes on Mousey.

Mousey let out a squeak of horror. We all saw what the monster was doing to our little buddy. He had already been through so much.

"Yeah. I ain't going through this crap again," said Red Beard. "Forget the mission!" yelled Red Beard. He aimed his antimatter slingshot. "Viieeuummmmm" went the weapon as it powered up. The creature sensed the oncoming threat and fired itself at the threat; claws sprung, fangs flashing and red eyes burning a deathly red.

"Poop" went the weapon and a warp field fired at the creature. Then 'zap!' Just like that; the creature was gone. All gone. There was nothing left this time, not even slime. The poop sound came from the collapsing atmosphere as the antimatter annihilated the creature and everything in its immediate sphere.

"I'll give it this, DelGato," said Sam. "The damn thing just won't be taken alive will it?"

"I guess not," I sighed. "That was our last chance of getting a specimen. Dang it!"

Just then, we heard "baaaaa," as a retarded-looking goat stumbled out from behind the barn. We all looked at it. It kinda looked at us but its eyes were crooked.

"It's possessed," chuckled Nikita.

"Yeah; by a retard," said Sam.

"Ah. You guys are a bunch of meanies," said Mousey as he approached the dumb goat.

"Baaaaa," said the goat as it turned to Mousey who had already stuck his hand out to pet it.

"There... See?" Mousey smiled. "He's not dumb. He's a good goat, aren't you boy? Come over... ahhh!!" cried Mousey as something was sucking his arm into the goat's mouth. "Kill it! Please help! Ahhh! Help me, please!"

But as Mousey struggled and flailed, the goat bucked. We were all aimed in but we couldn't risk killing Mousey.

"We don't have a shot, Mousey!" cried the big man, screaming as tears flew from his desperate eyes.

"Please! Ahhh," cried Mousey. "Please forgive me!"

He reached into his web gear and pulled out, then detonated his gravity grenade. In a flash, they were compressed into a ball of mush.

"Nooo! Dammit!" cried Sam. "Mousey! I should have at least done him that damn favor."

"No. It should have been me," cried Nikita.

"If there's anyone to blame, it's me," I said. "But right now, we gotta recover what we can and get this ordeal over with."

"Ha!" laughed Sam through her tears. "Looks like Mousey got the last laugh anyway. There's not much left."

"Yeah. Just my luck," I said. Secretly, I worried if what happened with the goat's DNA would happen with Mousey's. I dreaded recovering the biomatter but it was what it was.

FILE 5 BRAVO

The Drop

MY next orders from the red phone were clear. I had to write the entire file on old-school paper. No computers; no passwords, no hacks and no chance of any leaks. The Arecibo SCIF I was working in was pumped full of the sounds of hundreds of artificial typewriters, clicks, ticks and bings to avoid eavesdropping and decoding my typewriter's keys. I honestly still hear those clicking sounds to this day. Probably be the last thing I ever hear.

After a few weeks of typing the maddening files, I started to doubt the whole incredible thing, but I pressed on. I memorialized every detail until the final stroke of the final period had been pressed to paper. Before nightfall, I, along with what was left of the mess, was back in the air. The Blackhawk I rode on, ripped through the clouds at a furious pace. I've always liked riding on Blackhawks. They're like the Ferraris of helicopters.

As we transported the chupacabra files to Ft. Meade, MD, I looked around and I didn't recognize anyone. Other than me, not one original person was left. The five other people on board were Marines on security detail. All they knew was that a man with a suitcase shackled to his arm was on a mission.

At that level of secrecy, the phrase 'need to know' is used at every subsequent transaction. The number of personnel involved is dwindled down to the bare minimum, as often as possible until only the big dogs remain. The first big dog is the President and only a second-term president at that. You never know if the person elected is a maniac who just got lucky. Even the President's trust has to be proven when the stakes are so high. Next is the Secretary of Defense, then the Secretary of State, an obligatory witness (me) and the Chronicler.

The chronicler is the one secret person who maintains the codex of the United States. The Chronicler is the person with the longest institutional knowledge going back several presidencies. He or she has to be appointed by the bitterest of rivals from both sides of the aisle as to guarantee impartiality. The Codex is the narrative that contains our nation's, and most of our world's deepest secrets, disclosable only to a galactic-class power, should one ever reveal itself to us. A galactic-class power is any civilization advanced enough to cure or kill our planet in the snap of a finger, or tentacle.

But so far, there have been zero signals from the heavens indicating the presence of such omnipotence. Only greys and other strange, lowly characters have sent signals.

Signal analysis aside, due to increased monitoring capabilities, we also know that ever since the summer of

'47, we have had no other intelligences even close to our world, let alone enter it.

A short time ago, we learned that Einstein's prediction of gravitational waves was scientifically confirmed. Einstein reminds us that gravity, one of the four fundamental forces of nature, is intrinsic to all matter in the known universe.

So we, and by we, I mean not me, but a bunch of geeks and eggheads from more than 35 different countries, developed the Quantum Ultra-Integrated Lattice Security Structure (QUILSS) that encircles the entire planet. As Voyager I and II departed Earth in 1977 to spread the idea of exploration, science and existence throughout the universe, they secretly dropped off thousands of Quantum Lattice Balls (QLB) that are orbiting every one of the outer planets.

The Helios 2 Space Probe, which is the fastest ever human-made object, took care of the inner planets. Those QLBs act as quantum repeaters that stretch all the way from the sun's corona to the very edge of our solar system.

Just like the pair of black holes or merging binary neutron stars that caused the gravitational waves that confirmed Einstein's prediction, from infinitely far away, anything, and I mean anything that has mass, like little green men, giant energy blobs, robo-mechanical beings, gaseous bio-masses or giant purple people eaters that enter the local region of our world, will be detected. Even if they are traveling faster than the speed of light, the quantum nature of QUILLS ensures we will detect it.

In other words, if it can interact in any way with our version of the universe, QUILLS will detect it. And so far; nothing spectacular. Just boring old weird aliens.

So, for now, the Chronicler dutifully maintains the secrecy of the Codex. I learned a lot during that trip.

As the light of day broke over the horizon, I knew we had arrived at Ft. Meade when I saw the giant golf ball-shaped SCIFs on the sloping green knolls. Once we touched down, three of the Marines were relieved and only two remained with me. Shortly thereafter, I met the secretaries and the Chronicler. We drove the final leg, the Marines still fully armed for any contingency. It was only a short distance from the White House.

We dropped off the last two Marines in the lobby of the next seemingly random building and from there, we went underground. There was a gargantuan security hatch made of a mountain of titanium, steel and who knows what else. A loud, reverberating clang echoed behind us as we entered the last tunnel to the White House. Once there, I made my final briefing in the Oval Office. To my amazement, my briefing turned into a discussion.

I found out that my Earth-shattering discovery was not as important as I had once thought. It turns out greys had been visiting our planet for years. But the Big Dogs had never heard of one actually splicing itself with an

Earth creature, so they were very interested in how that happened. They told me that during the weeks I was in the SCIF, farmers all over Puerto Rico started finding their goats ravaged as if by some monster; a goat sucker or a chupacabra. But it's not the fully-grown chupacabra that ravages the goats. It's a maggot-like larva that feeds from the inside. And like the infamous Jeweled Wasp turns roaches into zombies, the larvae turn goats into walking food for the chupacabras-to-be. That's what killed Mousey.

"The reports from the farmers are becoming increasingly hard to explain with the usual stories of "he's just a crazy old farmer" or "it's a rabid dog that got loose," said the Chronicler. "The stories are becoming too difficult to dismiss."

President Bush seemed concerned. Even though Clinton had been selected, he was still a first termer. Bush, as the former head of the CIA, was beyond vetted.

"If this gets out, people are going to be very upset," said Bush. "For our country's and the world's sake, we need a plan to keep this under wraps."

"If I may, your honors?" I said humbly.

They all looked down at me but allowed me to speak.

"We have connections in Hollywood, right?"

They didn't seem to know what I was talking about but stayed quiet as if saying, 'Go on.'

"I've seen how quickly these things spread. I'm sorry, but it's impossible to contain. They spread too quickly. It's going to get out sooner or later."

The Secretary of State crossed his arms. "So why not beat them to the punch?" he asked. "You're saying to help these goat suckers spawn? Are you out of your mind?" asked the Secretary of State. "It'll be an international epidemic! The Black Plague of the 20th century will be on our heads. Absolutely preposterous!"

The other Big Dogs gave me an intense stare, allowing me one last chance to explain my thoughts.

"He wants us to just let these monsters loose on the streets and tell people to just get used to it?"

"No sir!" I said sternly but remembered my place. "I mean, sir, all we need to do is create the right image. Please hear me out. Right now, they are alien, goat-sucking monsters," I said.

"That's exactly what they are," said the Secretary of Defense.

"Yes sir. But what we need to do is create a character, a myth, a legend; one to rival Bigfoot, and the Loch Ness monster. People have been talking about these myths for years, yet no one takes them seriously, right? We need to create the next legend; one people will love to believe in, but also know deep in their hearts, that it's just as fake as the other monsters," I explained.

The Big Dogs looked at each other as if saying, 'Should we tell him?' But then they decided against it. I kept on as if I didn't notice, but after that, I was pretty sure Bigfoot was real.

"Our friends in Hollywood and the media owe us some very special favors. They will help us give birth to the next monster on the pantheon of legends… chupacabra!"

President Bush nodded in agreement.

"Make it so," said the Chronicler. "But while Hollywood, with all its tentacles, buys us time in the public eye, what about the creatures? You said so yourself, they are spawning out of control. It's only time before they kill another civilian."

"Sir, the good news is that chupacabras are not a threat to populated cities or suburban neighborhoods because there are no goats there. So, for now, and for the foreseeable future, the threat is contained. All I ask of you is to allow me to form a very special team and some time. Only with your support can I put a lid on chupacabra now and forever. However, I do caution. We will probably never eradicate it. Remember, it traveled more than 200 million miles to escape certain death on Mars so it didn't come here to die. But with your blessing, I'm confident we can contain it indefinitely," I said.

"Very well," said the Secretary of Defense. You'll have full disposal of whatever resources you need."

"I need the good stuff, sir."

"Of course. M-16s, 50 cals, Humvees…"

"Laser nets?" I asked. "Gravity bombs, antimatter cannons? I need the good stuff, sir. I don't have 30 years to wait and neither does the world, sir," I said.

"Uh-huh," said the Secretary of Defense. "Well, if you already know about it, it's all yours for the taking," he smiled. "Of course, with your permission, sir?"

Bush nodded. "Of course. Make us proud, son. But only us. You'll be the greatest hero no one ever heard of. Like the cunning Marty Cohen, the pernicious Richard Whisky or old Bob Bear, the ferocious."

"Who?" I asked.

"Exactly," said the Chronicler.

"I'll get with Mexico," said the Secretary of State. "They're the nearest country to California and besides, they owe me a special favor."

All the Big Dogs laughed a maniacal and disturbing laugh. I looked around and figured even at this top level, there were still and always would be more shadows to contend with.

"Good one, Les," said Bush. "Now, go make us proud, son."

We finalized our plan. And within the next two to three years, the plan came to fruition. We continued to learn as much as we could about our uninvited guests who just couldn't take a hint.

I told them not to worry so much because most chupacabras are the result of the crazy goat splice. They are small, feeble and shy. All they want to do is survive and are happy eating goats. They told me however that a subspecies had evolved; a sort of super chupacabra. Was the super chupacabra as a result of the splicing with Mousey?

The super chupacabras' real power is that they have advanced mind-controlling abilities. As we learned in Arecibo however, they can only control a mind that is not in control of itself. All a person has to do to combat the mind-controlling effects is never look into its eyes and then do simple math, over and over until the super chupacabra gives up. For the more religiously inclined, a learned prayer works even better.

I'm telling you this because chupacabras are real and if you or anyone you care for ever encounters one, you do not have to be afraid. Remember, they are just morphed, mutated greys.

It turns out Drake really did know something about humans, Martians and possibly all intelligent life. We are our own worst enemies. At some point, the Tower of Babble gets too tall and our intellect grows too heavy and we fall. Look at Mars; a wasteland. Even if the few, surviving Greys could take over our planet, it would be an exercise in futility as they believe we will soon destroy the

Earth just as they destroyed Mars. They are not trying to take over. Greys are just biding their time.

Despite their feeble nature, they did make it to Earth before we made it to Mars. After years of rudimentary communication with the Roswell survivors, the Phoenix lights and a few other instances, we have made an infinite leap in technology in only a few decades since that fateful crash-landing in the desert. July 7, 1947, changed our world forever.

FILE 6

The End

AFTER a deep sigh, the General, the man I had brought to the West Desert to teach, finally paused, as if to say, that was all he had left to teach.

"I don't know what to say, General. I'm honored. You bestowed this great knowledge upon me and I don't deserve it," I said.

"You're special," said the General. "I know you've heard that before. I know you are a good person. You'll know what to do with it when the time is right."

"I only have one question, if that's okay?" I asked.

He didn't object.

"How much longer do we have until we destroy Earth?" I asked.

"Who knows? Could be decades, maybe centuries. Maybe we'll figure things out for good. But instead of worrying about that, maybe you should use your energy to help our planet or create lasting peace. Who knows? The next galactic superpower might be you!" he laughed.

"Yeah. I guess there is a lot of work to be done," I said.

"Anything else? Last chance," said the General.

I debated over which last morsel I'd pick from his brain. Then I thought, 'Why not?'

"So, what tech exists today, that we don't know about?" I bravely asked.

"Well, if a galactic power shows up tomorrow, you'll be the first to know. I promise," said the General. "Otherwise, just survive for the next thirty years and you'll see for yourself. It's going to be great!"

Even though the night was too dark to even see my own hand in front of my face, I knew the General was smiling. I could hear it in his voice.

FILE 7

The Group

"RESCUE Beacon!" said an Agent over the service radio which I had cranked all the way up to level 12. I didn't want to miss traffic so it was very loud. "Rescue Beacon 99-51 for 2. Two hits."

The break in silence was jarring. I had already called it one of those boring types of nights where nothing happens. But then again, it was just a rescue beacon. No big deal. Probably just a quitter (an illegal alien who gives up and asks to be caught, usually due to exposure and lack of water).

"What does that mean?" asked General Delgado.

"Oh. It's just a rescue beacon," I said. "It's like a phone booth sized station with a big red button, an antenna and lots of water. If an alien was to give up, they just go toward the blinking blue light or the bright red flag depending on whether it's day or night, and press the red button. That sends a signal to our command and control room at the station and they let the Agents in the field know to go investigate. Now we just wait for an Agent to respond and if you want, we can go check it out as well."

"Yes!" said the General. "Let us go now!"

"Alright. Let's see if anyone answers up. Come on. Wait for it..." I said.

"10-4. Alpha 2-8-4," said Agent 284, whom I did not know. The Alpha stands for 'Ajo' for the Ajo Station and the 284 is his Star number which identifies him.

"Okay. So I'll let 284 know that we are PIO and that we are in the area and that we are going to respond and assist if needed."

"I got a body! Kooakotch MSC!" said the operator of the Mobile Surveillance Capability (MSC) that was located on a hill near the village of Kooakotch. An MSC is a million-dollar, high-tech, off-road 4X4 truck platform that uses radar, high-powered lasers, laser-range finders, infra-red (IR) and high definition video cameras as a system to detect illegal activity from miles away, day or night on the ground or even in the air. It also gives an exact GPS location so Agents can interdict whatever threat the MSC operator identifies. On the MSC's IR screen, people 'fluoresce' like white ghosts against a black background. Depending on the distance, the video quality can be detailed enough to see if a person is carrying a gun, a knife, a backpack or a bundle of drugs. And as a cherry on top, it has a digital video recorder (DVR) that records everything, at all times and cannot be erased so that it can be used for investigations or criminal proceedings if needed.

"He's running northbound from the rescue beacon," said Kooakotch.

"10-4, Kooakotch. 2-8-4," said Agent 284.

"Alpha 2-84, Tango 5-85," I said over the radio. I used Tango because I was working out of Tucson.

"5-8-5," said 434.

"I'm with PIO out of Sector. I got a 10-12 (important person) with me. Would it be okay if we 22 (rendezvous) with you on this traffic?"

"Hey, ah. 10-4," said 284.

"Break! Break!" called the Kooakotch MSC operator. "Kooakotch just picked up five, make that six, seven, eight more bodies!" MSC operators sometimes refer to themselves in the third person. "They're about 300 yards northeast of the beacon. It looks like they're headed toward the 26 Hills. Wait. They're grenading, (running in all directions). They just busted. Are there any Agents near their 20 (location)?"

"Negative. 2-84 is responding from FR-7 (Federal Route). I'm about 10 mikes out," answered 284.

"Tango 5-85 responding from Gu Vo," I responded. "Sir, get in the vehicle!" I ordered the General who was standing outside my driver's side window.

"Si. Vamonos!" he said as he ran around the backside of the vehicle and jumped in the passenger's seat and slammed the door shut.

I put the Suburban in drive and smashed the gas pedal all the way down. The white and green Suburban's wheels spun out and we jolted forward down the rutted out dirt road which was as wide as a four-lane road and just as straight.

284 was approaching from the north and I wanted to pinch them in from the south. As I was devising my strategy, the general yelled a very interesting question at me.

"What's chasing them?" yelled the General. He had to yell. A Border Patrol vehicle full of metal clanging gear, speeding down a washboarded road can get very loud. Add a radio at volume 12 and it can probably lead to hearing loss.

"What do you mean?" I yelled back.

"The MSC operator said there are no agents in the area, right? So why are they running?" asked the General. "They are about 10 miles from the highway."

"What are you saying, sir?" I asked.

"What did we just get done discussing? Chupacabra!" yelled the General.

"Oh. I don't think so, sir. They probably got spooked by javelina or a coyote," I assured him.

"Carajo!" yelled the General.

"Is there an Agent running behind the group? Kooakotch MSC," said Kooakotch. Crickets… "Hey, ah. There's something behind them. It might be the guide or… or something."

"Kooakotch, 10-9 (say again). Is it charlie? (cow or animal)," asked 284.

"Nnnnnegative," grunted a confused Kooakotch. "It's... walking on two legs now… It looks like, maybe a man. He's fast," said Kooakotch.

"A what?" asked the General.

"A man, you see? There are no chupacabras here," I reassured the General. "It's just a fast little Mexican."

"Kooakotch," called 284. "You should have me in your picture now. I'm getting close to those coords."

"2-8-4. 5-85," I called. "We just passed Old Manuel's Ranch."

"10-4," he replied. It's always good to let your partner know exactly where you are and where you are going and vice versa. Two armed agents unknowingly meeting each other in the dark is never a start to anything good.

"The group is still going full bore toward the 26 Hills," said Kooakotch. "That man is still chasing them. Wait, it looks like he's herding them. Wait. What the…?"

Crickets. Crickets.

"Kooakotch MSC, 10-18?" (are you ok), asked 284. Crickets. Crickets! "Kooakotch! 10-18!"

'Uh oh,' I thought. 'That's not good. I hope she's not dead or worse...'

"10-19, (I'm okay)," Kooakotch said softly. "10-19," she repeated. But her voice sounded different. The urgency was gone.

"2-84," said Kooakotch. "I got you in the same picture. Keep driving. Good line… Another 20 yards," said Kooakotch.

"10-4. Are they still running?" asked 284.

"Negative. They laid-up," updated Kooakotch. "585. Go ahead and get out on foot right there. You should be able to pick up their sign," she added.

"Come on, General. Get your flashlight," I said. I felt weird telling, not only a general but the great AmVictoran hero before me, what to do. I did, however, tell him, as I tell all my ride-along passengers that they needed to do exactly as I say, or their lives could be in danger. Some people, especially those who didn't particularly like us, got all huffy and puffy. But not the General. Even though he was a leader of leaders, he was at heart, a true soldier.

"284, keep coming. You're on a good line," guided Kooakotch. "585. Go in lights out in case they bust (run)."

"Stay close," I whispered to the General. It was one of those nights that had no moon. So essentially, I was running in a large, blacked-out closet with a sparkly ceiling; running blind, praying I didn't run into something with fangs, teeth or spikes. Most reporters would have freaked out. Light is their money. But not the General. He's been through worse.

"She saw something," the General loudly whispered.

"284's about to make contact," predicted Kooakotch.

A bright yellow cone of dusty light started bouncing around about 100 yards in front of us. I could still only hear our boot steps and my annoyingly loud breathing as we jogged as fast as we could toward the light.

I felt the sweat starting to bead up on the brow of my green baseball-style Border Patrol cap. 90 degrees at night is still 90 degrees. Since 284 seemed like he had a handle on the group, I was going to go lights on so as to not ruin a perfectly good cholla cactus bush or its tens of thousands of pristinely sharpens needles with my hot smushy body.

"One is running, 585!" warned Kooakotch. "He's headed right toward you guys."

I stopped. The General stopped right behind me. Embarrassingly, he was barely panting. For me, being in the PIO office and near all the best restaurants in Tucson, was not the best recipe for physical fitness. My heart was pounding in my chest and in my ears. I tried to close my mouth a bit and slow down my breathing so I could hear this guy.

'Breathe. Breathe,' I told myself. 'Slower. Slower. Good.'

"... su Madre!" said a muffled voice ahead.

"Alright 585. You should be able to make contact in about 10 seconds," said Kooakotch.

I pulled out my large flashlight, pointed it toward the grunts and clicked it on.

"Ah chingao!" screamed the man who looked just like a Oaxacan and he started running away. A Oaxacan is a small indigenous person from the state of Oaxaca, Mexico. The General looked like he was about to draw out his weapon.

"Stay back, General! I got this," I commanded.

The Oaxacan, whom I towered over, and I'm kinda short, was still moving away but in a ridiculous fake run at the speed of a leisurely stroll through the park. I couldn't help but laugh. I started to trot over to the Oaxacan and was within arm's reach in about one minute. My flashlight lit him up like a spotlight on a clown at the local talent show. He panted and howled, whimpered and whined. He dodged from bush to bush looking for a place to hide. I felt bad because he was seriously scared. At the same time though, he was doing the funky chicken and I couldn't help it. He must have heard a lot of bad stories about us. There are plenty of those.

"Parate, guey," I said as casually and non-threatening as l could.

"Baaa!" he screamed and 'hid' behind a scrawny bush the size of a large turkey. They have this trick where they close their eyes and look down. They figure 'if I can't see them, they can't see me.' Before you laugh, you should realize that it works more often than we like to admit. But when you actually see it and how pitiful it is, it's kinda funny.

"Okay dude. I can totally see you," I said nonchalantly in the Spanish language. He didn't budge. "Dude, if you don't get up, I'm gonna have to get you up," I warned a bit more forcefully. So the guy gets up and starts fake running again like a chicken with its head cut off. I gotta hand it to the guy he was very determined.

Alright, that's enough. I reached over and grabbed the guy's shirt and moved him gently to the ground. I placed handcuffs on him, mostly for his own protection from himself and sat him up.

"There. See?" I said snarkily to the General. "There's your monster."

"Don't kill me, please!" cried the Oaxacan.

"Hey," I called to him. "We are the 'migra,'" which is slang for Border Patrol. "I'm not going to hurt you or take your money. We don't do that here." He kept muttering and whimpering. "He's probably the guide," I said to the General. "The guides always abandon the group, hoping we go after the group and forget about the guide." Kooakotch and 284 kept chatting on the radio but by now the General was quiet and looking away from the light into the darkness. "General?"

"You don't feel that?" he asked me.

"Yeah. It's the feeling of satisfaction of doing my job. It feels great!" I exclaimed.

"Kooakotch saw something and this guy..."

"Parate," I commanded the alien who I didn't even know if he was Oaxacan. I didn't let the General finish. So he started cursing in Puerto Rican Spanish which they claim is more proper than Mexican Spanish, but that's a different story.

With a 'carajo' here and a 'mierda' there.

"284. We're making our way toward you with that one 15 (alien in custody)," I said.

"I'm going to interrogate him," said the General to me as if I had no choice.

"Parate," I commanded the alien. He complied. I turned to the General. Stuff was about to get real.

"Before we take him back to the rest of the group I just need to debrief him and get the intel and then I will let him go okay?" asked the General.

I just stared at him.

"I told you, this is why I'm here," he said. "This guy knows something and I'm going to find out what. This is very important, Diamante. Now, please! Let me do my job!" he yelled at me.

I stepped in front of the alien and kept facing the General straight on and said gently but sternly.

"There are cameras on us," I warned. "Remember. Kooakotch has been recording everything, including us, right now."

"Not anymore!" snickered the General. He made a quick move toward his waist belt.

Instinctively, I reached for my pistol. I'm a consistent expert shooter with a pistol and rifle. I was trained by two of the best marksmanship institutions in the world, the Marines and the Border Patrol. In short, I'm a dang good shot and a real fast draw. I didn't know why the General was trying to kill me, but I wasn't going to ask or let that happen.

No emotion. No thoughts. Just cold training. Before he was able to pull out what he was reaching for, my gun was already drawn, gun light on. His body was blurry and the tritium dots on my gun sights were crystal clear.

"Do not move!" I warned the General. I reached for my radio.

"Don't bother," he said coldly, as he squinted from the bright light in his eyes. "They can't hear you."

I squeezed the talk button on my radio.

"2-84, 5-8-5," I called. Crickets. "Kooakotch MSC, Tango 585." Crickets! I hate crickets! "960. 960 (our headquarters). Tango 585. Radio check... Anyone copy this radio? Tango 585."

"Gomen, baby," smiled the General. Just by hearing those words, I knew he had served in Okinawa. I also knew that the General knew more about me than I originally thought. Heck, he probably knew more about me than me. And now, I knew that he knew that I knew that... gomen basically means 'sorry.'

Even though he was smiling, he still hadn't moved. He knew me well enough to know that I would, in essence, stop the threat if I had to.

"I already did what I was going to do," he said. He could have been bluffing. "Look around you."

Look around is exactly what I didn't do. I learned the hard way, that listening to simple requests from adversaries is a bad idea. Like the time in boot camp when a Los Angeles gang member I hated, asked me to 'Come here,' as he lay in his top bunk. To prove I wasn't afraid, I got closer and he kicked me in the head.

Or the time when another recruit I was beefing with kindly offered his iron to me. I thought he wanted a truce, so I accepted it to iron my own uniform with it. Only after I had pressed the hot metal plate to my inspection cover (uniform ball cap) did I see the plastic melted all over it. He had sabotaged the iron which ended up ruining my best cover. 'Y'all got me,' I reminisced. But this fool is not going to get me. General or no General.

"Slowly!" I commanded.

"I can't see your face, much less your eyes," he told me.

My sights were still dead on and all the slack was pulled out of my trigger. I couldn't ask for a better sight picture. I was dreadfully calm.

"One by one, extend every finger from your right hand until your hand is completely open. Do not move your hand. Only extend your fingers. One by one. If you move your hand I will shoot you dead. Do you understand?" I yelled.

"Yes," he replied.

"Do it now!" I ordered.

He started to comply but kept talking.

"I am not a mind reader. I cannot read your mind but I know for certain that you have not looked at the sky. The stars are all gone. We are in a time bubble," he said.

"Now. Slowly raise your right hand high above your head. Do it now!" I continued.

He complied but kept talking. "That's why no one can hear you. Please remember everything I ever told you, I have a greater purpose and now, so do you. Please! Trust me. Just one peek and you'll see."

I hate to admit it but he made sense. Maybe I hadn't learned my lesson after all. I was about to fall for it again. I decided to peek. One quick peek. Besides. He could not know.

Peek. "Whaaaaat?" I gasped. What was flat darkness outside was now ultra illuminated. My eyes started slowly scanning and everywhere I looked I could see everything; trees, insects, snakes. If I desired, I could see a bright spec of a village far away and using only my will, zoom all the way in to see huts, people, license plate numbers, everything.

But I was only seeing the outline of whatever I looked at. A bright, rainbow-colored outline against a dark watery background. I looked up. I saw clouds, planes and even satellites. Had the moon been out, I'm sure I could have seen every dimple. I tried to zoom out, but there were no stars. 'The stars were gone? No. That's not possible,' I thought in my head.

"No. It is not," said the General.

I guess I wasn't just thinking to myself.

"It is a time bubble," he continued. "Would you please relax? I promise I will explain everything."

My mind must have been susceptible to hypnotism or at least the power of suggestion because my arms slowly started to lower. I didn't really want them to lower but I didn't really try to stop it. Instinctively, I holstered my weapon and un-blinded the General.

"Gracias, amigo," said the General. He slowly lowered his arms. "I can give you the details later. Right now, I just bought us some time. Doesn't this look a little familiar?"

"How could it? I've never seen anything like this," I said.

"Remember... The thing... The void?" he asked as if I should have known the answer.

"Oh, where the Chu..."

"Ahh, ah, ah!" he interrupted. He glanced over to the alien.

"What? The Oaxacan? He has no idea what we're saying," I boldly stated.

"You can never be too sure," said the General.

"Okay," I said sarcastically.

"We are cut off from the outside world and the outside world is cut off from us. Just like... Hehem. We can be here as long as we need too, so I can debrief..." explained the General.

"I already told you," I interrupted. "He's *my* subject, in *my* custody and therefore *my* responsibility. I don't care what he's seen. And I don't care how much time you bought us. We can be here until the end of time."

"You know how fast they spread," the General interrupted. "I already told you, if we miss our window of opportunity, we could be at fault for causing the next black death!" he pleaded.

"You cannot talk to this guy," I also persisted. "You have your protocols and I have mine. And right now, whenever now is, you're in my house, wherever we are. You're gonna have to find another way. Gomen, baby."

The General was really not ready to budge and he knew I was not playing around. My job is my life and the last thing I need is to jeopardize it for the General's curiosity who was not even sure if this poor guy saw anything anyway. He stayed silent but I knew the wheels in his head were sparking from how fast they were spinning.

"Besides," I reasoned. "When we eventually snap back to reality, the MSC's gonna…"

"The MSC!" he interrupted me back. "The DVR!"

"Oookaaay?" I said as if not really knowing what he was talking about.

"You are right, amigo," said the General. He touched something on his waistband and the field disappeared. Everything was soft, comforting darkness again and so I lit my flashlight.

I looked at the alien who was cringing behind me still looking freaked out.

"Get up," I commanded in English. The alien looked at me with a perplexed look in his eye. "Now!" I yelled. He whimpered and said to me "¿Quien, yo?"

"Diamante! He doesn't speak English," said the General.

"You can never be too sure," I smiled. "Andale. Levantate vato. Ya nos vamos."

"Alpha 284, Tango 585," I called.

"585," replied 284. So he heard me now.

"We're almost to your 20," I said.

"It was chasing us!" said the Oaxacan.

"What was chasing you?" I asked as we walked toward 284.

"A chupacabra, it took someone from the group," said the Oaxacan.

"A chupacabra?" I said. "You're crazy!"

"It was chasing us through the desert. That is why I went to the tower, to ask for help. Nobody was there to help us. It had already taken a person earlier and it was back for more people!" he said almost crying.

I started to have a feeling of dread. My heart felt heavy and I desperately thought something awful was about to happen.

"There," said the General calmly. "Do you feel that?"

"He's watching us," said the Oaxacan. "He's coming back for me!"

As he said that, I saw two evil red eyes flash from a thicket. Then, they vanished as did the awful feelings.

"What was that, General?" I asked. I was hoping for an answer and at the same time, I wasn't.

"There is a chupacabra out here on the loose," he said. "But don't worry. They never attack power. Only the weak," he gestured toward the Oaxacan.

We were only feet from 284 and what was a rather large group of suspected IAs.

"General, what about this guy?" I said.

"Would you believe him?" asked the General.

I chuckled. "Not in a million years. Go sit over there with the rest of the group, crazy," I said. The Oaxacan shuffled toward the group and sat down. They were all covered from head to toe with moon dust, a tan, light-colored powdered dust infamous in the west desert. 284 moved in and out of the group, showing no fear. He was a slim, bald-headed man with a serious face. His nameplate read 'N. Portman.' As he spoke to the aliens, in excellent Spanish for a non-native speaker, his tanned, weathered face remained expressionless. He was definitely salty (a senior agent who had many years of service).

"Tienen armas?" he asked the group. One from the back muttered "No." The rest kept looking down. "Cuchillos? Navajas? Drogas?"

"¡Que no, guey!" said one from the front. I quickly moved my light beam to his face. No way! The Oaxacan?

"That's Chuco Malo," said Portman. "At least that's what they call him. Yeah, he's really tough when he's abusing his defenseless sheep. Acts like a big man," said Portman. "But get him alone and he cries like a little baby."

"You know this guy, Portman?" I asked.

"He's a guide. I've personally caught him three times but he's in and out of here all the time," said Portman.

"Yeah," laughed the Oaxacan with a heavy Mexican accent. "It's true," he grinned. "Portman get me three times. But si. I make many trips. Now I need siesta and food," he laughed.

"Oh yeah he speaks English," said Portman. The General and I both looked at each other with an 'Uh oh' face.

"I hope the chupacabra get you!" screamed Chuco Malo.

"Yeah. He's always going off about chupacabras, and all kinds of crazy stuff," said Portman.

"Did you already search the group?" I asked.

"I was waiting for you two," said Portman.

"You!" I pointed to the Oaxacan. "Get up!"

"Okay. Okay!" he said as if trying to calm me down.

I grabbed him and almost picked him up off the ground.

"Ah, cabron," he yelled.

I gave him a hasty pat-down, and zip-tied his hands behind his back and put him in the detainment area in the back of Portman's kilo (pickup truck).

As I walked away I heard him scream "Chinga tu madre, guey!"

"Conocen a este vato?" I asked the group. Again, they were silent. "Hey, contestame!" I yelled.

The General said something in French; not quite yelling but loud enough for the entire group to hear him. They all looked up with a surprised, wide-eyed gaze and said in unison, "No."

"They are saying that they do not know that man," said the General to Agent Portman. "But I don't believe them."

"How rude of me," I said to Portman. "This is our 10-12. He's…"

"Officer Portman," said the General. "Hector Delgado."

"Pleasure to meet you, sir," said Portman. "How'd you know, that they, uh," he said as he shook his thumb toward the group.

"Take a closer look at them," said the General. Of course, I did too and I noticed the group was taller, a lot taller than the regular Mexicans; even me! Their moon-dust covered hair was short and curly.

"Haitians," declared the General. "I thought I recognized them."

"Great," said Portman with a big smile that revealed a bright set of perfectly white teeth. His bright blue eyes lit up from beneath the patina of his leathery face.

All of a sudden, he just cheered up. "So, can you help me out with writing and cleaning them up? (preparing for transport)."

"Oui," chuckled the General. Then he turned back to the Haitians. His voice deepened and he started speaking directly to the group. He paced in front of them as if he were pacing in front of a battalion. Then one stood up.

"Hey!" yelled Portman and me.

"It's okay," assured the General. "Trust me. He does not want to go back out there."

"Continuer," said the General in French. I understood that. The man who was about 6 feet tall and very skinny started telling a furious tale. His arms pointed and his hands made claw shapes. His face reacted to what he was describing. The General mostly listened and only had a few follow-up questions. Others in the group elaborated parts. The tale was short but intense.

"Were they telling you about how bad Chuco Malo treated them?" asked Portman. "He's known as a pretty bad dude around here."

"They were very scared, but they are glad to be in your custody now," said the General.

The General said a few more words to the group, this time pointing his finger at everyone, then tapping on his own head as he reviewed all of their faces one last time.

"Comprendre?" asked the General.

"Oui, monsieur!" they all said.

"I told them they are going to be safe now," said the General.

"Aller! Aller!" he clapped his hands. The group jumped up and started taking the trash out of their pockets, removing their shoelaces, belts and anything dangerous. They picked up all their trash, stacked their backpacks by the kilo and all got into it in an orderly fashion.

Portman flashed a pearly smile and let out a boyish giggle.

"Thanks, sir," said Portman. "You just saved me a whole lot of time. I'm not a very good mime!"

"No problem," said the General. "Oh yes. And tell your associates in Nogales they should expect Haitians over there very soon, probably downtown. They will no longer cross here. They say it is too dangerous."

"Thanks, sir," smiled Portman. "I'll make sure I do that, General."

"Great. It was very nice to meet you, amigo," said the General. "We have to be on the go now. Hasta luego."

"Where did you say you were from, again?" asked Portman.

"Eh. Puerto Rico," replied the General.

"Why did you come here to see what the Border Patrol does if you already have a Border Patrol station there?" asked Portman. "Ramey Sector. My buddy Portillo just got a transfer there."

Okay. I know he's rock-solid vetted, but that is a good question; other than the whole chupacabra thing.

"The Puerto Rico State Guard works closely with the Ramey Sector. We do a lot of joint maritime operations with them. In fact, it was they who pointed me to the West Desert," explained the General. "Right now, where you work Agent Portman is where the action is. And that makes the best training, tactics and techniques," said the General as he looked directly at Portman and smiled as he tapped me on the shoulder.

"Portman, good job with the group," I said. Another Border Patrol vehicle pulled up to the group. "I'll see you around," I said.

He was not smiling anymore. He didn't say anything. He just turned to the kilo and kept working.

The General and I made our way back to our vehicle.

"The MSC," said the General.

"What about it?" I asked.

"We need to go to it. I need to talk to the operator," said the General.

"Absolutely not," I laughed. "I already told you…"

"That was Chuco Malo!" said the General as he stopped walking. "I appreciate your commitment to protocols and to your job, but that was different. Now, you know why I'm here."

"I don't even know anymore," I said.

"We have reports from credible sources that many chupacabras are here but no one has been able to confirm it until tonight," said the General.

"Wait," I said. "You heard Portman. Chuco Malo is crazy and now we are all going crazy with him."

"Even more reason to get to the DVR," said the General. "That DVR on the MSC is all the proof I need. We need to mobilize quickly and you again are standing in my way."

"I'm sorry General," I said. "I already told you. I can't do..."

Buzzz. What the? I was receiving a call on my flip phone. This wasn't possible. I've never had reception this far in the middle of the middle of nowhere.

"Hello," I answered.

"Victor," said my supervisor, clear as day. "Is everything going well?"

"Yes, sir," I said. He had never called me during a ride-along.

"I just got word that the General's request to see an MSC just got approved."

I listened.

"It's kinda important to him, so if you have a chance, run him out to one of those out there and let him check it out," he said.

I listened.

"Hello?" he said.

"Yeah, yeah. Of course Robert," I said.

"Alright, bud. Thanks. Bye!" said Robert.

"Okay?" asked the General.

"You're good," I said with a smile.

I don't know who he was connected to, but he proved he could pull any string he wanted. We sped toward Kooakotch and before we knew it, the General was being briefed on the operations of the MSC...

"And that's how the MSC works, General," said Agent Stevens, aka Kooakotch.

"Thank you, Agent Stevens," said the General. "You did a very nice job with the group. But as we were running around, I felt like a character in a video game and you were the one who was playing the game! And since none of the bad guys got away, you must have gotten the high score."

Stevens laughed and looked a little embarrassed.

"Thank you, General," said Stevens. "I'm sorry I was confused about what I was seeing on the screen. I probably sounded like an idiot."

"No!" exclaimed the General. "You stop that right now! You kept everyone informed about the situation and you made all the right calls. If it wasn't for you, we could have lost half the group — maybe more."

"I tried being faster but I had a lot of trouble making sense of what was going on. I've been out here playing the same game five nights a week for six months straight. You'd think I'd be better at it by now."

"Have you ever played a game like tonight's game?" asked the General.

"Yeah. After a while they are all the same," she laughed nervously.

"Any new characters?" asked the General.

She furled her eyebrows and looked at me, trying to figure out what the General wanted.

"No," she said. "Why?"

"Why did the group first bust?" asked the General. "You said something was chasing them? Maybe a man? Maybe something different but definitely not an animal, right?"

She looked at me again. This time, worried.

"Don't worry," said the General. "You can tell us what you saw."

Now, Stevens really looked worried.

"Or wait. You can show me the DVR, right?" said the General.

She looked at me again.

"He is vetted," I said.

"Okay," she said. "I don't know what I saw. That's the truth. I'll show you. You can see for yourself." Stevens pulled up the file on the black and white monitor. It was mostly light grey with lots of light or darker shapes all jumbled. I could make out darker trees and mountains. The screen was panning back and forth as the camera recorded.

"Okay," she said, anticipating. "Okay. There he is, right after he hit the rescue beacon," she pointed to a white figure that looked like a small man, possibly Chuco Malo. "Okay. He's cautiously walking away from the Rescue Beacon. He might be the guide, checking if the coast is clear," she explained. "This is when the rest start to come out of the thicket. And just watch for yourselves.

"As the last of the group leaves the thicket, they are in a single-file line and very close to each other," she continued. "The darkness forces them to stay very close to the person in front or they risk getting lost or left behind.

I watched the group keep moving. Then, all of a sudden, they all stopped like a train hitting a mountain. They huddled, looking all around. One pointed and ran. The others waited. Then from the darkness crawled out an animal or creature. As big as a cow but shaped more like a dog with a long neck with the top arms clenched with what looked like large claws. It hopped toward the group and that was when they all started running in every direction. The creature jumped in the middle of the group and mixed in. Then it ran back into the thicket pushing random people back toward the center. It was very fast and jumped more than it ran.

As the people were corralled, they kept running the only direction the creature allowed them to run, northeast toward the 26 Hills. The creature would jump so fast from one side to the other it almost seemed like it was teleporting.

"Can you stop that right there?" asked the general.

Stevens tapped the keyboard.

"Back, like one second, please." said the General. "Okay, now play very, very slow," asked the General.

The creature lifted its front appendages which appeared pointy, almost like crab legs. Then it jumped into the air and vanished. A single frame later, it appeared on the other side of the group. It seemed to be teleporting. And if it wasn't, it moved so fast it might as well have been teleporting.

"This is where it gets weirder," said Stevens. "I've already watched it 20 times or more. It looks like it's morphing."

She hit the stroke of a key and the creature was behind the group once more but it slowed down and once again raised its appendages and its head, extended its hind legs and transformed into a figure just like the people in the group. It approached them. The group slowed down. It huddled with the group.

"You see how it gets closer to the last person and it kinda hugs that person who looks like a female to me. Then, the group scatters across this wash but the last two never come out," said Stevens.

"You see," said the General. "Chuco Malo is not crazy."

Stevens replayed it over and over. It indeed looked like something taking people into the darkness.

"Wait. Wait!" I said loudly. "May I?" I asked while I pointed my open hand toward the control station.

"Oh. No. Sure go ahead," said Stevens as she got out of the operator's chair.

"I used to work these," I said. "Are you in black hot or white hot?" I asked.

"Black hot," answered Stevens.

So I switched it and rewound the video then played it in slow motion. I noticed some activity closer to the edge of the screen where the wash led.

"Do you see that?" I asked Stevens.

"Yeah. It really shines out in white hot. It definitely has a heat signature but I still can't make it out," she said frustratingly.

I reviewed it several more times to no avail.

"What about the HD daytime camera?" asked the General.

"It's not daytime," I said. "Everything is completely dark."

"I used to do that too," said the General as he pointed toward the people on the screen.

I switched from infrared to the regular camera and started reviewing again. Then, I saw them.

"There!" exclaimed the General. I paused it. It looked like the same two glowing, red hot embers I had just seen with my own eyes.

"The eyes," loudly whispered the General.

I looked into the eyes. Fear gripped my body. I felt dread but also hate. "It's looking at me!" I cried out.

The General shoved me.

"It's an hour down," chuckled Stevens. I had snapped out of the panic but was still reeling at the horrible feelings.

"Now multiply that by a thousand," said the General. "I don't know how but somehow its gaze leaves a digital ghost of itself and can still affect you. I've never seen this before."

To save face, I replayed the event. I saw that the chupacabra's eyes actually project red light even in the dark and we caught its gaze right before it vanished.

"It knew something was watching it but they actually don't have very good vision," said the General. "Maybe that's why it vanished."

I stared, for too long at those evil red eyes.

"Wait. What?" said Stevens as she was piecing together what we were talking about.

"After this, you said you saw us, right?" diverted the General.

"Uh, yes," said Stevens still weary, but proceeded. "That's when this guy runs away from the group and you two get him. By the time I pan back, it was gone. After counting the bodies, I realized the group was down by one body," she said in the same quiet tone as before.

"I'm thinking maybe there was more than one scout and he did what all scouts do. He bailed," said the General.

"It's possible," said Stevens.

"And by the way he moved, it could have been a mountain lion," said the General. "I hear they are very fast and can get quite large. They can even be so quiet a person would not realize the lion is right next to them."

"It's possible," said Stevens.

"Keep scanning Stevens," said the General. "Oh. And great work!"

"Thank you, sir. And I will," smiled Stevens.

"Let us know if you see anything else," said the General.

We got back in the vehicle and rumbled slowly down the hill.

"Well," said the General. "I'm waiting for an apology!"

He was serious. I thought about it.

"I'm not exactly sorry, sir," I said. "I'd probably do it all over again, the exact same way, with the information I had at the time."

"Now that you know?" asked the General.

"I can't believe it," I said. Hearing you talk about it was one thing. But actually seeing a…" I paused.

"Say it," encouraged the General. "A chupacabra."

"A chupacabra," I said. "I just can't believe it, though. I guess it changes everything."

"Even to this day, I still can't believe it," said the General. "But knowing what we now know, we have to come back and put an end to this infestation before it gets out of control."

"What's your name?" I asked. He knew what I meant.

"Hector. Para servile," he answered.

"Hector, so you think it really killed a person tonight?" I asked.

"No," said the General. "How many dead bodies have you found?"

"Two," I said sadly.

"I'm sorry. But there are many more dead bodies out there, dried up in sandy graves. Their deaths cannot be explained by immigration. Our sources are reporting more and more signs of chupacabra killings. Now, with this," he held up a thumb drive. "We have all the confirmation we needed."

"Whose bodies are out there?" I asked naively.

"Illegal aliens? T.O.s?" asked the General. "Who knows? Who cares?"

"Nobody," I said.

"Exactly," said the General. "Because they are invisible. So nobody knows about the killings. But still, we have to win this invisible war in their forgotten names."

FILE 8

Before the Rains

WHEN I opened my eyes, I saw a lapis blue sky, powdered with paper-white clouds. A warm, moist breeze nudged the blue and white jigsaw puzzle northwest as I inhaled a nurturing breath of creosote and caliche clay. I always feel so peaceful before a monsoon, something like nirvana — like I finally understand. I don't know what. But I understand and it's okay. I feel good about it. How the petrichor from the coming rains blesses my body, my house, my neighborhood, the desert and the valley with its heavenly, earthy incense. I was standing on my front porch. I thought, 'I'd like to always be this peaceful.'

But then I remembered. That night in the West Desert, the General told me he had to prepare and get all the proper clearances for the upcoming extermination. He said they had to find a way to keep a war a secret. A shadow. But I still hadn't heard back from him.

It had been more than a year. How much longer did they need? People were dying. At the same time, I was glad I hadn't heard from him. I really didn't want to see him or his weird world ever again. It all seemed like too much. The burden was heavy on me. Knowing that chupacabras were out there, right now, on the rez. Invisible monsters killing invisible people. I wondered if they knew who they were targeting. Or, by the nature of evolution, they evolved into only killing people society would never miss. Either way, they stumbled across an ugly, unspoken secret and were happily feeding upon it. I don't know. Maybe I did want to see the General. I needed to do something. Lightning flashed far away.

The Arizona monsoons were coming. They are spectacular. World-famous for dazzling displays, danger and disaster. We know approximately when they will hit, but never exactly. Sometimes they crash us off guard. As if a sky gardener suddenly dumped a mountain-sized watering can over our heads. No build-up. No drizzle. Splash! Crash! Dry one second; drenched the next.

The purple, pink, blue and white lightning dances across the sky and zaps the earth with tremendous bolts. Its static branches spread like electric crystal fingers, propagating across the black glass of the sky. So many bolts, it reminds me of the plasma balls at kid's museums that you can walk up to and touch. Only in this plasma ball, we are stuck on the inside.

FILE 9

The First Drop

ARIZONA skies know when there are visitors in town. That day, they were showing off picturesque pinks, blacks, oranges, azures and reds awash in the west, following the setting of our yellow dwarf. A light raindrop splattered on my forehead.

"Aaugh. I hate getting wet. I hope they get here soon," I thought.

Stevens was pulling up to the parking lot at Sector in a silver SUV with blacked-out windows. Hector had recruited her after seeing her skills in action. He also made her his military liaison to the Border Patrol. I had always wanted to be a liaison but it wasn't my job. I had to stay in my lane.

I opened the passenger-side door to the SUV. Stevens was wearing tan cargo pants, tan boots and a form-fitting, long-sleeve camouflage top. A tan pistol rested on her hip. She was thin and fit. She had sharp blue eyes. I realized that I hadn't really looked at her that night on Kooakotch Hill.

"Oh. I'm sorry," said Stevens. "I was gonna get that."

"No, it's cool," I said. "I got it."

I reached to grab a tricky bag on the passenger's side floor.

"Oh, I'm sorry," she said again.

"It's cool," I smiled. I picked up the duffel bag and looked to the back of the SUV. A hand with red painted nails jutted out of the darkness.

"Give it to me, you," ordered the deep female voice.

"Oh. Here you go," I said, trying to act like none of this was weird.

The hand jutted out again and hovered. I shook it and then came the face. She was a middle-aged Hispanic woman with thick, dark eyeliner, shiny, raven-black hair pulled back in a military bun. Her lips were thin, slathered in rich, French-red lipstick.

"Special Agent Hernandez," she said.

"BPA Diamante," I reciprocated. I got in the vehicle and Stevens started driving.

"You the guy who drew down on General Delgado?" asked Hernandez.

Stevens gave me a confused look. I looked down and smiled. 'At least he doesn't keep secrets,' I thought.

"You're not too smart," barked Hernandez. "General Delgado *let* you do that. You know that right?"

I cleared my throat.

"You drew down on the General?" said Stevens with a confused look like she was bewildered but somewhat impressed.

"You kinda had to be there," I said. "It was a misunderstanding. Kinda."

"Ah. At least you got cajones," said Hernandez. "I'd rather work with someone like you than half of these pansies who just do what they're told."

As soon as we passed the guards at the front gate to Davis Monthan Air Force Base, Stevens hit a button and let go of the wheel. Her seat spun around toward me. All our seats relocated to form a sort of roundtable. All the windows turned into screens with dim orange graphics and information.

"We've been reconning the area for weeks," said Stevens as she gestured across the orange graphics. A holographic map popped up at the center between us.

"We've confirmed at least 20 suckers. Possibly a hundred or more larvae," said Stevens.

"Suckers?" I asked.

"Suckers," responded Hernandez. "Second-strain mutation."

I must have looked puzzled.

"Chupacabra!" shouted Hernandez. "Regular-type chupacabra. You know, the famous ones with the spikes and red eyes. They're the spawn of the second strain that fused with the DNA that came from Mousey. It's the strain Kevin and his weirdos reanimated. But there other mutant strains as General Delgado explained to you?"

"There's a third type," added Stevens. "We're not sure what it is or what it does. We haven't been able to confirm. Whatever it is, we expect its DNA to be very different."

"Are there more strains?" I asked. "I mean, if the greys fused with a goat, then with a human, can it fuse with other animals? Contrary to popular belief, there are a lot of animals in the desert. A lot!" I emphasized.

"General Delgado said there have been reports of other types of creatures; creatures never before seen by the locals; worse than suckers," said Stevens.

"So, how are they different?" I asked.

"I don't give a rat's butt how they are different," said Hernandez. "We're gonna make sure we get rid of it before the population explodes. No matter what, we're going prepared for anything."

I nodded in agreement. Again, I felt privileged that they picked me to help.

The SUV kept driving itself through the base heading toward the hangars.

"So. You were a Marine?" asked Hernandez in the most incredulous manner. Like she couldn't believe how *I* could have possibly been in the illustrious Corps.

"Yes, Ma'am," I said.

"You ready to move that fat around?" asked Hernandez as she pointed to my beer belly.

I felt a bit hurt because it was true. I was kinda fat. I had put on quite a few pounds since I started working in an office environment. I knew I gained weight because I had recently compared photos of my early days on the Field Training Unit (FTU) with recent photos of me in PIO. My face still looked young but chubby. At least I knew where to get the best tacos.

"Yeah," I laughed. "But I can still work, though." I hoped I was right.

"We're going to meet with General Delgado tonight near Quitobaquito Spring," said Stevens. The orange map before us zoomed in on Quitobaquito Springs.

"Why so close to the border?" I asked. "You can literally throw a stone and hit the fence (with Mexico. NOT a wall)."

The SUV came to a sudden halt. Stevens' seat rotated back forward as her window rolled down. Stevens stuck out her arm and waved her RFID card. A gate opened and we proceeded to drive toward the flight line between the immense hangars.

We pulled up to the flight line where a C3-1A was standing by. It's a midsize propeller plane. By this time it was drizzling. I hate getting wet. We all grabbed our gear and scooted into the bird, strapped in along the sides of the cabin and sat on the green, cot-style seating area.

We put on our helmets which are also communications devices.

"Please secure everything, ladies and gentlemen," said the co-pilot. I read 'Sean Hall' on V-VIDS (Visual-Visor Informational Display System). V-VIDS was the latest experimental tool that was being tested on all special ops communications gear. He was from North Carolina and a major in the National Guard. Relatively young but again, an impressive collegiate athletics resume and exceptional flight and law enforcement experience. The bird immediately started taxing toward the flight line.

"Teresa," said the pilot in the standard scratchy, Midwestern pilot voice. I knew it was night, but I pictured him wearing mirrored aviator glasses. As the passing runway lights shone through the windows, I saw Hernandez's face light up and she displayed her white teeth behind the red lips. The plane accelerated. She was seated behind the cockpit and couldn't see the pilot's face but looked in his direction anyway with that big cheesy smile.

"Last time I saw you was at YPG (Yuma Proving Grounds). You were still testing GAUs on LAVs (light armored vehicles) back then," said the pilot.

"And you were still flying the Golden Knights around, Roy," said Hernandez. "I hope you're a better pilot than you were back then."

"I only crashed two birds," said Roy. Sean said nothing but kept pushing buttons and doing co-pilot stuff. We were airborne.

"Three!" laughed Hernandez.

"Drones don't count!" yelled Roy smiling.

Were they serious? I hoped we didn't crash! I hate flying.

"You can't learn to two-step standing in a square, can ya?" said Roy. He pulled up on the controls and the plane shot vertically like a rocket ship. As I struggled to turn my head toward the window, the Christmas lights and glittering globes that blanket Tucson in all colors at night tilted and twisted as we zoomed away across the sky. I guess I could never be Santa. I don't have the stomach for it.

"Don't worry, y'all," said Roy. "Mr. Hall here is the ying to my yang. Isn't that right Major?"

"Yes, sir," said Hall nonchalantly. "I'm the yin," he corrected respectfully.

I turned back and the glitter was just a glow beyond the horizon. Soon enough, we leveled out and were coasting.

"I thought you said you were never going back to Yuma?" said Roy.

"I haven't been back," said Hernandez.

Yuma? We were going to Yuma? I hate Yuma! I said the same thing about Yuma. I never wanted to go back to Yuma. I have so many horrible memories of Yuma. It's only three feet from hell. Of course it's Yuma. Only bad things come from Yuma. It practically is hell!

"Yuma?" I asked nonchalantly. "I thought we were meeting at Quito," I said as not freaked out as I could. I looked at Stevens.

"We are going to Quito, but we can't go in through 85," said Stevens. "We'd be spotted by the suckers too easily."

"Also the cartel scouts," said Hernandez. "They're always up high, glassing (observing) in all directions. They got tech now. They'd give up our 20 in a heartbeat."

"We're en route to Fortuna Mine," said Roy. Fortuna Mine is the crater of a dead volcano in the middle of nowhere that was explored for natural resources, but nothing ever came of it. Now, it's just the scar of the activity of humans who have long since died. I had actually driven through there a long time ago on a 4X4 expedition of El Camino del Diablo, the Devil's Highway.

Fortuna Mine is located near the beginning, or end, of an offshoot of El Camino del Diablo, which is an infamous, 100-mile-long desert trail from Yuma (hell) to Ajo (almost hell) through a scorched landscape similar to what you would see on Mars. Temperatures regularly exceed 120 degrees Fahrenheit or hotter. The trail is littered with graves and crucifixes marking the agonizing end of many doomed and misguided journeys.

There are a handful of secret tanks that hold water for a few days out of the year. After it rains, those tanks can be accessed for the life-giving liquid, only if you know where to look. But, since it only really rains during the monsoons, most of the year, they are just hollowed-out rocks containing little more than moon dust. Other than that, water is virtually nonexistent.

"El Camino del Diablo is a long way from Quitobaquito," I said. "It'll take us at least two days to get there from Fortuna Mine. Unless you know something I don't know, there's no way we'll make the rendezvous with the General tonight at Quito."

"We'll make it," said Hernandez.

"I've driven to El Camino. We won't make it," I warned.

"Diamante," said Hernandez. "We are going to fill you in as needed. The team has been working things out for a few weeks now. Trust me. This is the best way. You do trust me. Don't you?"

The plane continued.

"I just met you, Teresa," I answered.

"No. No. No," Hernandez said. "You cannot call me Teresa. Only my friends call me Teresa. You just met me. You are not my friend. You got that?" yelled Hernandez.

"Sure thing, Hernandez," I said sarcastically.

"Not yet," said Stevens smiling and trying to diffuse or deflect. "Maybe we can all be friends later, right?"

"Thanks, Teresa," said Roy.

"Tu, callate," yelled Hernandez at Roy. You could hear Roy laughing over the intercom.

"No. This is not the best way," I protested. "The General told me everything. We had a deal that we would be open with each other all the way. You're asking me to go in blind while I'm risking my life? No. I'm out."

"And the General's right, Diamante. I agree with you. But we're not really holding anything back from you," said Teresa. "We just think it's going to be better for you to see for yourself. I also agree with Teresa. We are going to make it to Quito," giggled Stevens.

"I don't think so," I said. They were all giggling. They did know something.

They kept reminiscing and talking but I zoned out. What did they know? I stared out the window into the darkness. The plane steadily hummed.

After a few minutes or a few hours, I heard a voice bring me out of my thoughts.

"Is everyone suited up?" asked Roy, back in his pilot's voice. Hernandez and Stevens replied with a "check." I thought about it.

"Check," I replied like a sulking teenager.

"Mr. Diamante," spoke the co-pilot for the first time. "Look out your window, sir."

"Okay," I said.

"See the wing?" he said.

"Okay," I replied.

It was just a fixed-wing. Big deal. But then my eyes jumped wide open. My forehead bumped the cold glass as my head tilted forward in amazement.

The wing started to ripple like a bedsheet at tuck-in time. The humming ceased. The plane tilted and started diving like a dart.

'Okay. This is it,' I thought as I closed my eyes. 'Main thang never panic. Breathe.'

"Diamante," called someone.

I did not want to see them. There was nothing I could do about the fact that I was about to die, but I didn't have to look at these strangers.

"Diamante!" yelled Hernandez. "Abre los ojos," in her non-native Spanish. I know. Here I am, about to meet death and all I can think about was her technically correct yet not quite proper pronunciation. Also, if she was Hispanic, why was she not proficient in Spanish? Is that racist?

"Mr. Diamante," said Hall in a calm and reassuring voice. "Look out the window again, sir."

Fine. What was once a static fixed-wing aircraft was now two wings fluttering at an almost invisible speed. I turned back to the interior of the aircraft and it was no longer a military tube. We were inside a fluorescent orange and green glowing organism. I reached up to touch my face but the V-VIDS was already covering my face and providing breathing air. It displayed all the same graphics as in the SUV as well as incorporated the 360 degrees as well as X-ray and infrared vision.

Everywhere I looked I saw orange strands of information and tiny graphs. It was all too much at first. But I soon found I could keep it just out of mind, enough so it didn't interfere with my consciousness. Soon it all but disappeared. I knew however that if I wanted it before I could look for it, it was already there.

We were sitting in different body parts of what could best be described as a giant dragonfly. Roy and Hall were seated at the helm in the reflective geodesic eyes. Roy controlled the brain and Hall controlled the movement. I felt their connection, acting as one synchronous mind in charge of flight.

Hernandez and Stevens were in the thorax in charge of internal mechanisms and threat assessment. I felt their collective movements were completely effortless and in unison like the powerful yet graceful legs of a ballerina flowing through a symphony.

I was in the butt.

The mech suit I had previously donned had morphed into the same glowing molecular material as the organism. The bright, light colors reminded me of the colored plexiglass that we used in shop class to make red and pink hearts for our moms and girlfriends.

I was in a seated position, facing forward but suspended. I felt safe, warm and dry like I was inside a plastic bag that was tightly surrounded by medium density goo. I wiggled my fingers and I suddenly felt the organism's wings flutter. I froze. I didn't want to move and alter the organism's flight path.

"Don't worry, Diamante," said Stevens. "You won't change the dragon's flight path."

'Could she read my...'

"Yes. She can read your mind," said Roy. "We all can."

"Great!" I thought. All of you can read my mind but I can't read yours. Of course."

"We are not stopping you," said Roy. "You are stopping you."

"It's only readable when it pertains to the entire organism," said Sean. "You gonna need to meld your mind with the machine to make its body seem like your own. We can only communicate about our shared connection through the machine. But don't worry, Mr. Diamante. We can't read each other's personal thoughts," he giggled.

"Yeah. I bet he's happy about that," said Hernandez.

"What?" I asked. "You should be happy you don't know what I'm thinking about you, Hernandez."

"I don't give a rat's butt what you're thinking about," she whipped back.

"Come on now y'all. I don't think any of us want our personal thoughts being read," chuckled Hall.

"We have about 30 minutes left before we descend," said Roy. "Diamante, I'm going to ask you to explore your connection to the EEMO, (Extrasensory Experimental Mechanized Organism) as if you were flying the dragon yourself. I'm activating your training matrix, so feel free to really build the mind-body connection."

"And keep your eyes open," added Sean. If you close your eyes for too long, you lose your connection."

I quickly jolted my entire body and shook it out to a full extension and back to the seated position. I felt the entire dragon (I guess that's what they called the dragonfly machine) jolt in response. I flexed my back muscles and I felt each of the four wings beating. I twitched and changed the pattern. My body, or the dragon, rose and fell as my slightest whim made it zip this way or that.

I didn't have to do much. Most of what was happening was as if the dragon was on autopilot. It reacted to wind gusts and floating material almost by instinct.

As each minute passed, I gained better and better control, as if I had been born a dragonfly and had been one all my life. I recalled the muscle memory of skimming a pond, the choreographed movements to fly through a forest of reeds. My mind scanned my environment for predators and prey. I was recalling my hunting instincts.

I was discovering the speed and agility needed to catch mosquitoes, moths, other dragonflies and even small fish. I was controlling the pitch, roll and yaw as quickly as you imitate a flying bug with your hand.

"We've been able to reverse engineer a whole lot of organic tech from the craft at Offutt (air force base)," explained Roy. I understood him perfectly. As clear as the deepest conversations I've ever had in my life. It is almost impossible to understand how many levels of confusion are added to every conversation we have ever had. Everything muddles communication. Things like setting, relationships, ulterior motives, biases, innuendoes, assumptions, miseducation, fears, hopes and drives all alter the communications we send and receive. It is a miracle we can understand each other at all!

But some conversations are crystal clear. One expresses. One understands. Another expresses and is understood.

This is the way Roy was communicating with me. Then I discovered I was using what seemed to be two brains or two consciousnesses. I was learning to maneuver the dragon and listening to Roy at the same time without any distractions. I was 100 percent focused on both at the same time.

"The General said the craft crash-landed at Roswell," I stated.

"It did," said Roy. "That's why everyone thinks the aliens and craft are at Area 51. We let them believe whatever they want. People love myths. They believe it so strongly, I wouldn't be surprised if people tried to storm Area 51 one day to see what is there."

"So they are at Offutt," I deduced.

He did not refute.

"Out of sight, Out of mind," I thought.

"Correct," stated Roy.

Meanwhile, my other consciousness was enthralled with the new machine. Straight up. Zip! Straight down. Zap! Ninety degrees right. Zoom. Ninety degrees left. Zam! Lightning-fast forward. Whip! Full stop. Whack. Backwards. Bam.

Normally, the G-Forces would have turned my body into jelly. But the pressurized goo enveloping my body and whatever other tech was at play kept me intact and awake. Only when I pushed the dragon to maximum speed did I barely get the acceleration sensation like jumping off a high diving board or riding on the back of my uncle's motorcycle.

I could even swivel the dragon up and left and then right and down and then up again like the smooth, swinging motion of a pendulum. I swung the dragon in a Ferris wheel motion, tracing the perimeter of a wheel in the sky. From the perspective of a bystander, I would have appeared to be zooming by like a corkscrew. Amazing!

"So, I guess you're in?" said Hernandez.

"Maybe," I joked. She knew I loved it. Then, I realized she was sharing her mind power with me so that I could experience the multiple consciousnesses required to operate the dragon. One could do it alone, but it's more effective with another person.

"The dragon is the most complicated EEMO in our arsenal," said Hernandez.

"And the most difficult to maneuver," added Sean. "The rest are super simple to operate compared with the dragon."

"So there are others," I deduced.

"Correct," said Hernandez.

I couldn't read her mind past the dragon connection, but I felt the gravity of her experiences.

"Desert Storm," she said.

"When the world was really ending," said Roy.

"It's always ending," said Hernandez.

I felt the clarity of her intentions. They were simple. She wanted only to teach or to learn. She did not like to be taught. And she wanted to be part of our team and finally to win. I had no further reason to fear her.

In the training program, my kaleidoscope eyes caught the glint of lightning about five minutes away. I knew time. I had never experienced controlling such high velocities, much less being able to quantify them with numbers. In other words, I had no idea how fast we were going in knots or MPH or anything. I felt a wave propagating around the dragon's skin as it zipped through the sky. The wave felt fragile as if it was on the brink of snapping like the crack of a whip. We were flying beneath the clouds, just under supersonic. Sonic booms are not good for things that are trying to hide.

Above the soggy clouds, the sonic rumblings of thunder quivered my gossamer wings and vibrated my antennae as we drew nearer. I realized the dragon was vulnerable. No force fields. No magic armor that can repel lasers and bullets alike. It was tough and would withstand a serious beating. But it was not impenetrable. I had to rely on tactics and the art of war.

The best way to win a battle is to never get into one. Well, that option was gone. We were headed for battle. The next, best technique is to obliterate your enemy before he realizes what's going on hence the utmost need for stealth. I felt a single cool raindrop on my face. I wasn't sure what we were getting into, but we needed a good plan. The General wouldn't let us down.

FILE 10

El Camino del Diablo

THE rain continued. The wind was gusting but the dragon was steadily hovering directly above Fortuna Mine, but at the height of Mt. Everest. From that altitude, the dead volcano looked like a burn mark on a golden bed sheet.

"Diamante," yelled Hernandez. "You're going first."

Aaugh. I hate getting wet.

"Stevens," she continued. "You're going after Diamante. Shawn, you are after Stevens and I'll pull up the rear after Shawn. Roy. I'm sure we'll see you soon."

"Not too soon I hope," said Roy. "I already need a break from you!" he laughed.

"You butt head," laughed Hernandez.

"Alright, Teresa," laughed Roy. "Y'all clean up this spill before we have to save the world again. Take care darlin'."

"Go! Go! Go!" barked Hernandez.

I let go of my will to remain in the dragon and since I was still seated in the butt, I slipped out of the safe bubble wrapping grip of the dragon and my warm body smacked the cold thin air mixed with fat raindrops. It basically pooped me out. I felt the rain, but the suit was not getting wet. Even with the upgraded suits, my hot blood was shocked by the freezing air rushing past my body. I was supposed to look for Fortuna but I turned around instead. As a hurled downward, the suit started warming up and normalized my body temperature.

I saw the dragon quickly shrinking away as I plummeted. Stevens' white suit shot out of the dragon. Like an Olympic high diver, she somersaulted and twirled with style until finally deciding on a spike position. She shot through the air and quickly caught up to me. I checked my timepiece, we had plenty of time. Hall and Hernandez practically did a tandem, jumping almost at the same time.

Stevens and I kept looking up as if we were on a giant bed of air. Hernandez quickly caught up. She pointed to her eyes, then pointed straight down. I turned around and I could see Fortuna clear as day with my V-VIDS. It was barren. I checked my altimeter and we were at 12,000 feet. At this speed, we were smacking into the rain instead of the other way around. We were all splayed out to cause maximum wind drag and slow our descent. Still, Fortuna was growing quickly. I wondered if the rain would affect the chutes?

When I jumped with the Golden Knights, we opened our chutes at 10,000 feet and we were quickly dropping to that elevation. I reached for my chute and Hernandez gestured 'stop' as she shook her head. Was she crazy?

"You don't need your shoot," she said over V-VIDS.

"Then why do we have them?" I asked.

"Get in spike position," she answered.

"What!" I yelled. We were supposed to be slowing down not speeding up!

Hall and Stevens immediately rotated to spike position and quickly dropped.

"Devil Dog! Catch up!" shouted Hernandez. I was definitely not like the General. He was always in command. People were always telling me what to do.

On top of that, she Devil Dogged me. I haven't been Devil Dogged in more than a decade. Reluctantly, I spiked my body as we hurtled toward the volcano which was larger and larger by the millisecond.

Without even realizing it, I saw on my V-VIDS that we had less than 30 seconds before joining the original Fortuna miners.

"Together!" she yelled. I maneuvered toward the group. They were huddled together. I reached them and huddled in. We were still in spike position. The mine was five seconds away. I had to pull my shoot now or die. My heart raced at 200 bpm (beats per minute). I looked down. Eyes open. Oh, well. Good Marines don't disobey orders.

Wham! The ground opened up and whoosh! We punctured the surface of some green, bubbly goo that filled a deep void in the mountain.

I grasped and grabbed two of my partners as our tremendous force kept pushing us deeper and deeper. I didn't know whose gear I was grabbing but we all held together. My V-VIDS was giving me information but my brain wasn't responding. When we ceased descending into the goo, I gently felt solid ground forming beneath my boots.

"Just relax," said Hall in his deep but calm voice. "It's doing what it's supposed to."

I still held onto my partners who were all covered in green slime. I blinked. We were alive. Our suits began to glow. I was standing. I stepped forward. The goo just slipped off my suit. My V-VIDS cleared.

"We have two hours to get to Quito," said Hall. "The doggies are ready. Are all of you ready to integrate?"

"I'm ready to poop my pants!" I said.

Everyone started laughing. I was in shock.

"What just happened?" I asked. "How are you all fine with this?"

"Moving on…" complained Hernandez.

"Yes, sir," said Stevens. "We are all proficient with the dragon so the doggie should be a piece of cake." The platform raised and a path lit before us. My eyes followed the path to something I had never conceived.

With roughly the same dimensions as a gigantic construction dump truck, was what looked like a biomechanical ground squirrel sitting in one of the large rock caverns. It had angry glowing green eyes and thick sharp claws. It was another EEMO. Its skin was a sparkling light orange hue that was almost transparent. It sat ready on its enormous haunches. Each of its four paws was as wide as a manhole cover. It waited. Ready, but still...

"A ground squirrel?" I said out loud.

"Oh!" said Stevens as if she had forgotten something then cleared her throat. "Hhhe, hhe, hem. Despite their cute and amusing appearance, the Sonoran ground squirrel is actually one of the most powerful and impressive mammals on Earth," as if she had memorized the fact.

I just stared in sarcastic disbelief.

"To scale!" she added.

"Like that makes it any better," I said. "It's a freakin squirrel!"

Several operators who were already at Fortuna started assembling around us.

"The squirrels are going to be the main combat platform against the suckers," said Hall. "It's loaded with an array of weapons specialized against the suckers. Its exterior skin is radar-absorbing and virtually bulletproof."

"Virtually?" I muttered.

"We don't expect the suckers to be shooting .50 cals, Diamante," said Hernandez.

No one laughed.

"Why not?" I said. More operators gathered, nearly a dozen.

Hernandez gave me a death stare.

"That would actually be kinda cool," I said with a dumb grin.

Everyone laughed.

"Have you ever seen anyone die from a .50 cal, Diamante?"

I had messed up again.

"Have you!" she persisted.

"No," I admitted. Everyone's smile disappeared.

We kept walking toward a silent swarm of giant EEMO ants. Their skin was candy apple red, with metallic flakes glittering as the light changed.

If you ever take time to look down at the micro-world of ants for a second, you will see that they are amazing in so many ways.

For one. They all agree on a purpose and do whatever it takes to make it happen. Humans can't even have free face painting without some jerk cutting in line. Ants do not have that problem. Everyone has a role and dedicates their life to it.

Physically, they speed on the ground. They virtually glide, over rocks, crevasses, plant life, and any obstacle. Sometimes even do so while carrying something like 50 times their body mass and going literally straight up a wall. No one trips. No one falls. No traffic jams. No gridlock. No rubbernecking. We will never achieve such greatness as a species.

Finally, ants are fearless. When I was a kid, we used to pit different insects against one another in a coliseum of death. Our gladiators were black widows vs hornets (sans wings). Scorpions vs centipedes. Tarantulas vs wasps. But the best, most epic warriors were ants. The most epic of battles were the hordes of red vs. black ants.

They would attack by the dozens and engage in a giant ball of combat, agony, death and glory. Actually, ants would win against any adversary, as long as there were enough ants. My favorite ant battle was the ants vs. the Bruce Lee scorpion.

While playing in the waterless Santa Cruz river, I was digging into one of the sandy banks for fun and to my great pleasure and surprise, out popped a baby scorpion. Baby scorpions are notorious for being super aggressive and for the massive amounts of venom they deliver during combat strikes.

I quickly found a plastic cup and scooped it up. All I needed was a worthy opponent. I searched under rocks, sticks and bushes but I couldn't find anything, not even a stink bug for target practice.

Finally, I settled on an ant hole. The black ants in it were busy scurrying about at a peaceful yet busy pace. I dropped the baby scorpion near the center of the hole and it immediately started racking up kills. Its tail shot forward like a bullwhip on rapid-fire. Clueless ants were left twitching and trembling in its wake. The many dead bodies started to fill up the entrance to the hole. The scorpion would fire in all directions the way Bruce Lee used to fight many opponents at once and arise victoriously. The baby scorpion started moving away from the hole toward the outer perimeter which was less densely populated.

Then, the ants realized they were under attack and their movements became more frantic and super speedy. They charged at the scorpion but it held its ground. The ants were relentless. They did not hesitate to hurl their bodies at the scorpion who would dispatch them in a millisecond. The scorpion's aim was deadly accurate to the micrometer.

Then, inevitably, it missed. An ant was able to grab one of the baby scorpion's legs. The scorpion turned its attention to the ant but it was too late. Before it had the chance to address the ant, 20 more were within killing range. Not long thereafter, the Bruce Lee scorpion belonged to the ages. The ants remained undefeated. If these EEMO ants were half as relentless as real ants, the suckers were in real trouble.

"These are the scouts," said Hall.

"Scouts?" I thought. "We need soldier ants, not freakin' scouts."

"They can be switched into soldier mode if needed but their main mission is recon," said Hall. "If you are assigned to a scout, go ahead and get ready. You'll be launching in about 10 mikes."

'Wait,' I thought. 'I don't know who or what I'm assigned to yet. Great.'

"Diamante," said Hall. "The General wants you to be with Ms. Hernandez as part of the first wave," said Hall.

'Even better,' I thought sarcastically.

"If you can fly a dragon, controlling the scouts is gonna be easy for you," said Hall. "Also, be aware. There will be AI (artificial intelligence) scouts within your swarm. Their minds share a strong link, almost as a collective. And just as dragons fly through the air, scouts fly on land."

"Canyon, mountain, hill, thicket, whatever," said Hernandez as if she was annoyed with me. "Nothing will get in your way."

"Just as ants go looking for food, you will locate targets, then communicate the location back to the hive. Once we know their location, we will come in to finish the job with the doggies. Since we only have a handful of doggies, we need to be efficient with the extermination," said Hall. "That makes yall's mission critical."

"And we will make it to Quito in one hour," stated Hernandez. She stamped her boot three times on the deck. "That is 2200 (twenty-two hundred) hours." She stamped her boot again, sending booming echoes throughout the caverns. "You are a collective. There are no individuals. Mission accomplishment. Got it!" she stated.

'Uugh,' I thought.

We kept walking. The cavern was an endless spider's web of tunnels carved out of solid rock. Every tunnel or crevasse showcased a different type of EEMO.

A loud zapping buzzer echoed about the caves. Dozens of more operators in mech suits emerged from the corridors. Each person's suit was different. Some were made of a fabric material like a dazzling Indian kurta. Others were robotic and metallic looking. All different colors and textures, but all had glittering bioluminescence underneath. All had retractable face shields and fully integrated into each individual.

"The General had handpicked each person for their abilities," said Hall. "He paired each operator with an EEMO that fits their mind and body like a glove." I noticed my suit had turned a brilliant red.

The EEMO operators assembled around Hall who was standing next to a copper mountain lion EEMO. It too was sitting on its haunches but it was not as massive as a doggy. Still, it was even more menacing. Its sparkling copper skin was almost holographic in appearance. Its giant razor-like claws were visible under the translucent skin of its paws.

"Each one of you guys and ladies is cross-trained on at least one other EEMO," said Hall. "Every EEMO can be operated by any one of you. But you will have to let it know who the main operator is. You do this with a hard reset. The hard reset locks you in as the main operator and as long as you are the main operator, no one else can operate your EEMO. Y'all got it? Good."

Hall walked toward the head of the beast, looked into its two jeweled eyes as if he were taunting it. Suddenly, the lion opened its enormous jaws and swallowed Hall in one gulp.

We were astounded. What had just happened? The lion shook its powerful head and neck then stood on all fours. It reached out to stretch and pulled back its giant metal claws at the polished concrete floor, leaving eight deep broken gouges. The lion quickly turned its head to look at the crowd.

"Now that's what I call a hard reset," said Hall over V-VIDS. Everyone laughed with him.

"Alright listen up. Right now we got temporary control of every RVSS, (remote video surveillance system) and IFT (integrated fixed tower) tower from here to Tucson. We've tapped into the MSCs, and any other tech capable of spotting us; that we know of, let me say," said Hall. There was a slight laugh.

"We've notified Border Patrol, TOPD, BLM (Bureau of Land Management), Fish and Wildlife and all other friendly actors out here that we are gonna be performing military training for the next 48 hours. However, we need to wrap this thing up before sundown. We just bought some extra time in case we need it. Y'all feel me?" asked Hall. Everyone nodded and smiled.

"Luckily, it's gonna be raining out there, so we also expect minimal cartel activity. We're hoping for some real heavy flooding. If we don't get it, we're gonna have to give nature a hand if y'all know what I mean. I'm telling y'all if there was ever a time to exterminate, the time is now." Operators looked at each other quietly nodding.

"But this is our one shot. We can't wait 'till next year, y'all. By that time, it's gonna be too late."

"Scouts!" yelled Hernandez.

'That's me,' I thought.

"Move out," ordered Hernandez.

Hall gave Hernandez a sideways look. "Everyone else, come with me," said Hall.

Now I felt lost. But that wasn't a new thing. It wasn't a big deal. I learned that with good leadership, I can figure out anything and sometimes even without it. I followed Hernandez. V-VIDS read 'T. Hernandez - Scout Cmdr. (commander).' She was a strong leader. Only a hand-full of human operators were following behind her.

"The rest of the scouts are AI," said Hernandez. "The swarm is going to learn from your successes as well as your mistakes. They are very fast learners and will soon surpass your abilities as operators. Make sure you have more wins than losses," she said as she turned to me.

I hate being singled out. She was getting on my nerves.

She stood in front of an EEMO scout and stared into its eyes. The scout twitched then opened its mandibles and devoured Hernandez in one gulp. The scout twitched again and turned its body toward the rock wall. On the scout's abdomen, was written "Suck it, suckers," accompanied by a large pink heart written in greasepaint. Hernandez was tough but always a lady. The EEMO link was active.

The garnet swarm started crawling up the rock face behind Hernandez. A few of the other scouts were personalized too, some with shark teeth drawn around the mandibles like the airmen who draw on the noses of A-10 Thunderbolts and other aircraft. Another scout had an obscene hand gesture and something horrible in Spanish. One said "See you in hell," on one side and "See you in Yuma!" on the other. One was adorned with beautiful kanji symbols. I doubt they meant anything beautiful. If I survived, I might personalize my scout, too.

Hernandez's scout climbed effortlessly, then upside down, as it followed the contours of the rock. Finally, it reached the top and a hole opened up and the garnet swarm disappeared into the night. A curtain of rain poured in before the opening closed and left me behind.

"Diamante!" yelled Hernandez. "Hurry up!"

I focused on creating a link with the scout. Intense situations, I tend to focus on one thing and take things step by step.

I stared into the empty black eyes of my scout. I saw a thousand reflections of my face. I tried to focus on one. My face slowly started swirling. Zwap! Before I could have my next thought, I was in the scout. I was an ant. I looked through the volcano as if it were made of cold crystal ice. I felt the heat of ancient lava deep beneath my feet.

I saw my brothers and sisters spread away in all directions like grease in a pot when a drop of soap splashes in. My dense body felt incredibly strong and extremely fast. My feet felt magnetic as I magically climbed vertically and even upside down over an outcropping. I crested over the opening. Through technology, I saw the vast sea of hills and valleys before an infinite horizon.

Mountains are powerful monsters, containing eons of love, hate and most dangerously, indifference. They've killed many men mentally and spiritually before killing them off completely. Such an impossible journey across horizons of hills is daunting enough to deter any human. But in my scout, I felt superhuman.

I turned toward Quito. I raced to the bottom of Fortuna and across the wet desert floor. My V-VIDS showed the other scouts' locations, progressing like the shadows of a fleet of airplanes racing up and down hills and forward at the same time.

Nothing got in my way. I saw a canyon approaching. It was as deep as a skyscraper and just as wide. At the bottom were house-sized boulders among the sand. Normally, I would have gotten on foot and carefully made my way. But the scout made easy work out of it.

Out of curiosity, I opened my mandibles and grabbed a chunk of one of the boulders. With some effort, I lifted it and secured it in my giant jaws. I raced toward the other canyon wall and made it up the side with no problem. I threw it aside and kept crawling the cragged mountains. I was going about a mile every 12 seconds. Or about 300 miles an hour. Not faster than a jet but faster than I had ever traveled on land.

I veered off the mountain range that parallels El Camino del Diablo onto the open, flat desert grounds. I went a little faster on the ground but not enough to make a difference. So I veered back toward the safety of the mountains.

"Diamante," called Hernandez.

'Oh, no,' I thought.

"Yeah," she said. "Get on it."

I switched to infrared, radar and bio-detection spectrums. The bio-spectrum picks up common signs of life like methane and carbon dioxide emissions. I climbed to the top of the peak in front of me. I started scanning. Nothing. I climbed to the next. Nothing. I climbed to the next. I looked at my V-VIDS for a second. I saw a hint of violet fumes emanating from the peak of another dead volcano about a mile away. Aside from desert life skittering about, there were no other significant life signs on my spectrums. This was promising.

'I'm gonna go check it out,' I thought.

"Wait," said a deep but soft voice. I thought I recognized a hint of a Native AmVictoran accent. I paused. I looked for his profile on V-VIDS. Q.A. Young - Sells Cmdr. He was Tohono O'odham and an active Shadow Wolf. He had an impressive resume including two tours in Afghanistan and action all over the world. He was a real AmVictoran hero.

'What am I doing in company like this?' I thought. 'I have no place here.'

"Did you check around on the other side?" asked Young, politely.

"No," I said embarrassingly.

"There might be a scout," he added.

"I didn't think about that," I continued.

"It's okay. We're a team," replied Young.

"Diamante," said Hernandez from about 20 miles away. "I told the General, you have no combat experience. Your combat training is more than a decade old. Heck, you don't even like playing violent video games," said Hernandez.

"What's your point?" I said.

"You shouldn't be here, on this team, on this mission," said Hernandez in a non-hostile tone. "I'm not trying to be mean but you might get yourself or one of us killed, Diamante. You don't want that. Do you?"

I looked down.

"No," I confessed.

"Patricia," said Young. "I can look after him."

"You know that's not true," fired back Hernandez. "This is life or death. There is no 'out of role' or 'ceasefire' now. You mess up and it's game over. No extra lives," said Hernandez.

"Remember, I don't like video games. I don't believe in extra lives," I said.

I launched the scout forward and around the ridge I was on.

"You can still go back," yelled Hernandez. "No one will judge you."

"No," I said plainly. "I'm here for the General, not you." I maneuvered to a better vantage point. I got in a covered position. I scanned the other side. Sure enough. There it was, bright as day on my V-VIDS. A lone chupacabra scout was perched near the top. After a few seconds. It crawled around to the other side.

"I almost made a mistake," I said. "It won't happen again," I grunted.

"I'm here if you need me, buddy," said Young.

"Shut up, Quentin," said Hernandez.

I quickly dropped down to the valley then up the mountain that the chupacabra was on. I had to make my way to its new location without it noticing me. I silently approached. I saw it. Its back was turned toward me. I knew it was going to return to the other side to continue scanning. I found a crevice and backed up into it. I waited.

"This is just like Border Patrol work," I thought.

"Only when you catch him, you're not going to give him water and crackers," joked Young.

"Kill it," said Hernandez. I wasn't sure if she was talking to Young or me.

"Both of you," said Hernandez.

"Can you stay out of my head for a freakin' second please?" I yelled. There was no reply.

The hairs on my legs and body sensed it approaching. Even through the furious rain, I smelled its stench with my antennae. Rotting meat and dragon breath whipped away from the chupacabra as the wind blew it right at my mouth. I saw it slowly crawling in front of me, back to its original post. I stared directly at the back of its head. It abruptly stopped. It turned its head to look at me. I launched, not giving it time for any shenanigans. My pinchers grabbed its body. It was wiry.

Even though I immediately knew that it was no match for me, I felt that it was extremely strong. Had I not been in the EEMO, it would have ripped my natural body to shreds. Luckily, the situation was the other way around.

In only a few milliseconds, I maneuvered its body so that it was inverted. I injected my needle-like stinger right through its forehead into its brain. It instantly went limp. I noticed a small red inverted square pop up on my V-VIDS with a two next to it. My first confirmed. I looked straight up and saw a red inverted square shoot up like a superhero beacon to the clouds through the gusting wind and rain. Now, everyone knew where the den was.

I knew from working on the MSC that a red inverted square is the NATO symbol for an enemy. A blue horizontal rectangle stands for a friendly, green square stands for neutral and a yellow popcorn symbol stands for unknown.

Now, to find out what the sucker was guarding.

I approached the opening with caution. I deployed a nano drone that was about the size of a poker chip. Again, I was not even aware I had that ability until I needed it. It materialized from my thorax and then launched into the unnatural crevice that was only about 20 feet deep and extremely cramped. As it maneuvered deeper into the crevice it scanned with all the same spectrums as a full EEMO. It immediately spotted a broken, portable solar panel next to a bloody handheld radio and a couple of smashed cell phones. The walls of the crevice were stained with blood as if something had been slaughtered in there.

Meanwhile, I was outside huddled back in my crevice. The nano scout's video was live in our shared consciousness to whoever wished to see it. I sensed all the other EEMO scouts, including the AI and Hernandez, were tuned in, frozen with curiosity.

"Those look like cartel scout tools," I said.

"Yeah. But why would they..." said Hernandez when the nano scout saw the dried out, empty carcass of a human male. His eyes, still in his skull, only completely white like two marbles. His face was permanently frozen with the look of unspeakable fright. The cartel scout's death was recorded as another red inverted triangle for an enemy death.

"I told you to stay out of my head. Especially right now," I said.

"Wait, wait, wait," rattled off Hernandez. "You spoke to us first. That meant you were opening the lines of communication," said Hernandez.

"Shut up!" I yelled at Hernandez. Again, silence.

Now. The chupacabras had been targeting the cartel scouts. But why? At least we found out why illegal alien apprehensions had decreased so rapidly. All this time we thought it was a result of political policies. Of course it wasn't. Chupacabras make more sense.

The nano scout then quickly picked up the source of the life signs. Five disgusting, wet chupacabras were huddled together like rats at the bottom of the hole that the cartel scouts had probably dug out by hand. When the nano scout zoomed in on one particular sucker, its eye opened. Maybe it sensed that it was being watched, like the one outside. The others awoke and started licking their mouths like rabid chihuahuas. After a second of seeing nothing, they reluctantly laid back down.

I thought, 'Nothing more to see here.'

I recalled the nano scout, picked up the dead chupacabra and continued forward toward Quito. I dropped the carcass into a river that had formed in the wake of a monsoon flash flood.

I had seen many monsoons in my days, but this one seemed especially ravenous. Lightning struck. The storm's hate was growing.

In a few minutes, the casualty counter went up to four. An AI-EEMO scout had located another chupacabra den about 15 miles north. I looked to the dark sky and saw another beacon go up.

I rushed forward, hilltop to hilltop, scanning all the while for more dens. Then I saw another beacon go up, then another and another. The AI scouts were using my experience to find other hidden dens. Maybe my being here was not that crazy after all.

The enemy counter on V-VIDS which was at 10, separated into two smaller red icons. The red circle with a dot in the middle was for the five probable cartel scouts who had been wasted. The other red saucer shape represented the five suckers we wasted. Luckily, the blue friendly and the green neutral symbols remained at zero. No friendly deaths and no neutral deaths. So far.

My EEMO scout rushed over the ground like a hurricane. I followed the Camino, knowing it led to Quito. Before I knew it, I was at Pozo Nuevo road, 14 miles north of Quitobaquito.

Hernandez, Young and the rest of the scouts had already spread out.

"We've scouted all the way close to Tucson," said Young. "There's no suckers east of the Babos. But 86, west of Sells, is flooded out."

"Good!" I said. "That's going to prevent any more civilians from entering the war zone," I said smartly.

"Floods are also very dangerous," said Young. "T.O. brothers and sisters die in floods every year."

'I think I'll just keep my mouth shut,' I thought.

"There's nothing north of Why," said Stevens.

"We know there's none west of Fortuna," said Hernandez.

"South?" I asked.

"Well, we can't go past the borderline dummy," said Hernandez.

"Dummy!" I yelled. "You're the one with the Sharpie eyebrows," I jabbed.

"Actually," said the signature, fake-deep English voice in a theatrical tone over V-VIDS. "My sources say that there is a presence all the way south to Banori (a small smuggling ranch in Sonora, Mexico, not far from the border)," said the voice.

"General?" I said with excitement.

"Of course, Diamante," said the General. "Were you expecting Pancho Villa?"

Everyone laughed. I hate laughs at my expense. Especially when girls like Hernandez and Stevens were present. Hernandez laughed the hardest. Of course she did.

"Where are you, General? I don't see you on V-VIDS," I asked.

"Where did I tell you to meet with me, Diamante?" answered the General with another question.

"Quito," I answered annoyingly.

"Then that's where I am going to meet with you," he said. He was smiling again. I could hear it in his voice. Was he laughing at me?

"Well, hurry up Diamante," said the General.

I jolted the scout forward and down the peak I was on. Up, down, up, rock, tree... The desert flew by my EEMO as I scurried toward Quito. Then, as I was dropping into a canyon, I saw a shadow shoot up from the ground, beyond the hill in front of me. When I crested, I saw it drop into a canyon beyond a hill in front of it.

I went faster to catch up to it. But it kept its distance just out of my reach, going hill over dale.

I activated soldier mode and immediately I realized a whole array of weapons, all ready to fire. I couldn't take any chances.

'No extra lives,' I thought.

Suddenly, it stopped at the top of a ridge and faced me. I quickly approached, ready to fire. Then I heard "That's it!"

It was the General in a suit! I climbed down then up to him. I dropped out of the EEMO.

He grabbed me and gave me a giant bear hug. He growled like an old bear.

"Rrrawr," he growled. "I knew you were gonna come back, Diamante. I knew it. That's why I pick you, man. You see Teresa? I told you."

"Relax, General," said Hernandez from somewhere near Gu Vo. "We just got here. There's plenty of time for him to screw up, again."

"Thanks, Teresa," I said mockingly.

"Oooh!" she screamed. "You're lucky I'm not there."

That's the reason I was mocking her.

"Hhmm, hhmm, hhm," giggled the General.

I happened to glance down. I looked for his leg. It was gone. I stopped laughing. He noticed. He looked at me staring at his robotic leg.

"You never disappoint me, Diamante. You guys see this guy? I love him."

"Hector," I said. "What happened to your leg?"

"What do you mean 'What happened to it?' I was just syncing it out here on the Camino. I think it's working pretty good, no?" he laughed. "The knee was not responding, but now, it's better than ever." No one on V-VID was chatting. They all 'looked away.' The awkward silence grew loud.

"Yes, sir," I said. "But what happened?"

"Don't be rude, Diamante!" scolded Hernandez. "It's none of your business. That's all you need to know."

"It was a great mistake that could have been avoided. It's something that never should have happened. But, it is what it is," concluded the General.

"Okay," I said.

"Come on! We're almost to Quito," he said as he bolted forward.

Since I was already synced with the scout, it instantly swallowed me up, almost before I asked it to. I rushed forward. A few hills later and we made it. I looked at the time: 2200 hours.

FILE 11 ALPHA

The Eight Hour War

THE General was standing tough next to a black EEMO scorpion, glittering like crystalized stingray skin. On the side, it read 'Los Escorpiones Negros' and flew a painted PR flag on the stinger. Its giant pincers were open and ready to shear anything to pieces. Its tail was elevated high, the needle was sharpened to a microscopic point.

A purple lightning bolt struck behind him. I looked around. I could see why the General picked Quito. Even though it was in the middle of the middle of nowhere. It was also in the middle of all the strategic targets. The base at Fortuna wasn't the headquarters. The headquarters was wherever the General stood.

"I feel like fighting," he whispered. The scorpion whipped its tail as if to strike the General down. It vibrated its pincers and the body shook. It lowered itself to the ground and slammed the pincers at the General's feet. He stepped onto a pincer and grabbed the tail. The scorpion lifted the General and gently placed him on top of itself. The General vanished into the scorpion.

The General stood up on his hind legs and raised his pincers toward the sky. He released a guttural scream that rattled the mountains. Two, then three and four bolts struck his glittering exoskeleton.

"Who is ready to kill with me?" yelled the General.

Suddenly, I became enraged at the invader-murderers.

"This is all wrong," I said over V-VIDS. "I shouldn't be out here. I should be back home with my family, on the other side of the horizon. Instead, you monsters come to our world for hope after scorching your own planet. How dare you!"

I raised my two front legs and opened my mandibles. I let out my own guttural scream. Lightning struck my body and I felt exhilarated!

"Haven't I heard that somewhere?" asked Teresa sarcastically.

"Shut it, Teresa!" I said. "Not now."

"You have haunted my dreams," screamed Young. "Killed my people with your empty thirst for blood. How dare you!"

I saw lightning strike about 20 miles north.

"These people are suffering!" screamed Stevens from the Growler Mountains up north. "Invisible people are dying!" she cried. "Entire villages are collapsing. How dare you!"

A giant asymmetric electric spider web splashed across the purple-black clouds in the sky. Lightning struck again; orange this time.

As scores of operators acknowledged their inner anger and hatred for the extraplanetary scum, the sky basically blew up with hatred and lust for revenge. It left a giant hole in the sky with no clouds. The dazzling sky shone once more over our heads. It stopped raining. Silence.

"We know all of the targets," said the General. "Everyone is in position. All of the elements are active. The war zone is closed. No one gets in. No one gets out. Fortuna?"

"Yes, General," said Cmdr. Gonzalez at Fortuna. "Standing by, sir."

"Then let slip the ground squirrels of war," commanded the General. I got chills. So did my EEMO. "Scouts, activate soldier mode," he continued.

'Finally,' I thought. I realized my light arsenal. I felt plasma blasters at my disposal. But they were not turrets. They were potentialities possible of erupting at any point my consciousness needed them to arise and shoot. Onboard AI would handle the rest. I felt invincible.

"Easy! You're not a soldier. You're just a glamorized scout, Diamante," said Hernandez. "All of you remember that. The doggies are the main fighting platform."

At the same time, she uttered those words, a bright explosion lit the clouds west of Quito. I looked at the casualty count, it jumped from 10 to 15 in one hit, then 20, 25. It kept going up. I stopped counting.

My exoskeleton turned black with only slight hints of crimson. I felt my exterior harden from flexible plasticity to hard, yet light armor, similar to the ceramic ballistic plates we use against heavy fire.

"Move out!" screamed the General.

I launched forward. I saw a target. Just like before, I dropped low and circled around. As I was preparing to go in and waste the suckers, I saw a giant doggie fly past me. It was in mid-flight as it dove headfirst into a chupacabra den. Its face was lit up with bright orange and blue war paint. It came out with three suckers scratching and screaming but it shook its powerful neck and ripped their bodies apart, flinging limbs across the mountain peak.

As it ripped them apart, in slow motion, I heard the doggie operator. "There's two more inside toward the bottom. You can finish them off if you move now!"

I noticed I had never lost my momentum and continued toward the den. As soon as I saw their signatures, I unleashed a barrage of plasma fire into the den. Vaporized sucker meat and melted rock fumes exploded out of the cavern. I gave no time for fun or games.

I glanced back at the doggie operator. V-VIDS read 'N. Portman - USBP liaison/combat team.'

I smiled.

"Welcome back, Portman," I said. "Couldn't stay away I see."

"That crazy Oaxacan wouldn't shut up about the chupacabra and I kept asking questions," said Portman.

"So they figured they couldn't shut you up, right?" I added.

"It was either this or a promotion so I guess they figured this was cheaper!" he chuckled. I laughed with him.

Before I could finish my chuckle, both my antennae lasers fired again toward Portman. My AI had picked up two suckers in mid-air trying to attack him.

"Woh! Jeez!" screamed Portman, still laughing.

We continued fighting side by side. Our taste for war grew sweet. As the fires lit up the hills, shadows of monsters slaughtering monsters projected against the rocks like a gruesome puppet show.

The pause in rain prompted smugglers, waiting for days to finally move their illegal cargo. Days' worth of illegal aliens anywhere from China, India, El Salvador, Israel, Cuba and of course Mexico, started flooding across the U.S. border into the West Desert. Behind and in between the sacrificial lambs, came the evil drugs.

"Fortuna!" called the intense yet respectful Portman.

"Portman!" called Cmdr. Gonzalez.

"Sir, we need to stream relevant video feeds to Border Patrol ASAP, sir!" said Portman.

"10-4 sir," said Cmdr. Gonzalez. "Relevant Border Patrol feeds are hot! If you see anything that needs tweaks, let us know, sir," called Cmdr. Gonzalez.

"Gonzo," called the General. "Make sure our operators can see that video cone."

"Already done, sir," said Cmdr. Gonzalez. "EEMO operators! Stay out of the way of those sweeping video cones. We don't need any unauthorized inquiries as to our existence just yet."

I looked up and saw the RVSS and IFT towers had lit up the desert like a tapestry of lighthouses. The light beams narrowed and widened, swept and pointed wildly and unpredictably as Border Patrol operators tried to coordinate the apprehension of hundreds of IAs and drug smugglers creeping across the border. Some groups had already made it well past the border into the interior of the United States.

"Do not engage!" yelled Hall. V-VIDS now read 'Special Agent S. Hall - FR-21 Cmdr.' "I repeat, do not engage IAs or drug mules. Border Patrol and OA (other agencies) will handle. Stay on mission."

I literally had to hold myself back by digging my legs into a rock. My instinct was to chase, especially evil drug smugglers. 'There were too many bodies for the Patrol,' I thought.

Just then, V-VIDS picked up six objects coming in hot from the east. I zoomed in. There were six Border

Patrol agents. Three on ATVs and three on dirt bikes. They moved like a pack of lions. The video cones followed the illegal movements and the agents started to round up the groups.

"My people got this!" snickered Portman.

"I never had a doubt," called Cmdr. Hall.

"General, we have activity on Banori, just as you warned," called Hernandez. "Reports say suckers are popping up out of the ground attacking humans, goats, whatever!"

"Take care of it, Teresa," said the General

"I wasn't asking for permission, Hector!" she said. "I'm taking two AI scouts and I'll need a doggie," she called.

"I ain't got a doggie but I got a kitty that's itchin' for a fight," called Hall from his mountain lion. "I'm already east of you, Teresa. I'll meet you at Christmas Gate."

"Commander Hall. That's what I like to hear," called Teresa.

"Teresa," called Young.

"Go ahead, Quentin," said Hernandez.

"I have people closer to Cmdr. Hall. They can help him right away. I'm seeing less activity over here out east. It looks like all the activity is shifting west your way."

"You got it, Quentin, I'd rather be near the action anyway," said Hernandez.

Young, in his silver wolf EEMO stayed close to the top of Baboquivari Peak, the most sacred place in the T.O. universe. The T.O. believe their creator, I'itoi and their people sprang forth from this holy mountain and that the spirit of I'itoi is active and present. Devout believers, like Young, still converse with I'itoi as they walk among him. He dispatched a doggie to meet Hall at Christmas gate and secure Bonori.

Hall stood by his mountain lion at Christmas Gate. On V-VIDS, he saw two AI ants quickly approaching as well as a doggie. He peered out with his eyes and saw the ants sweeping in, but he had no visual of the doggie. In a flash the AI scouts were standing by, ready for a command. Hall saw that on V-VIDS that the doggie was supposed to be within a stone's throw away, but he still had no visual. He felt the ground tremble beneath his paws and jumped up like a scared cat as the doggie popped out from under the ground.

"Woh!" said the young operator. "These things are super diggers." Enter M. Turner — Special Forces — Combat Team. He had baby blond flat top hair, light skin, bright blue eyes, a sharp nose and thin, stern lips.

"That shouldn't be surprising," said Stevens who was fighting skirmishes out of the Growlers toward Dead Man's Tank. "They are modeled after the excellent digging ground squirrels."

"How's it looking over there, Estephanie?" asked the General.

"The doggies are already here hitting most of the targets," said Stevens.

"So we knocked them out? Great work, Stephanie," said the General.

"I'm sorry, sir," said Stevens. "But we're finding most of the targets have been abandoned. All of our signs point east."

"Thank you, Estephanie," said the General.

"That's not all, sir," said Stephanie. "AI picked up about 40 possible campers and hikers still out on the Organ Pipe Cactus National Monument (OPCNM). At least five different groups spread out about 35 square miles."

"Notify BLM, give them an accurate headcount and exact GPS coordinates for each group," ordered the General. "And before you move east, make sure you don't miss even one sucker. It only takes one to start a whole army again."

"Yes, sir!" replied Stevens. "I'm on it."

Within seconds, AI scouts had emailed the data to BLM as well as generated robocalls with the same information. Stevens started locating groups of campers. But for one group, it was too late...

All but one of the groups camping out in the OPCNM were snuggled, sleeping safely in their tents. The westernmost group, however, was a group of students exploring the wild west and they were telling scary stories.

FILE 11 BRAVO

The Campers

SABLE lay on her cot, pulled out her cold damp feet from inside her red sleeping bag and splayed them out before the crackling fire.

"Why is it so cooooollllduh?" she whined. "It's the desert. It should be like steaming hot right now-ah."

"Aren't you from Scottsdale, Sable?" asked Zaden.

"Ah yeah," Sable answered.

"So you should know that clouds are basically like our sky blanket. No clouds, no blanket. That's why it got so cold all of a sudden after that weird burst of lightning."

"Oh," complained Sable.

"And I've known people from Scottsdale and Phoenix and no one talks that way," said Zaden.

"You see all those strange lights?" asked Hawk as he pointed to their horizon. Taylor, the girl he wanted as a girlfriend listened as did the four other campers huddled by their campfire.

"Those are UFOs," said Hawk.

"Haaawwk," whined Taylor. "Stooooppppaahhh. You know that kinda stuff scares me."

"No, I'm serious," said Hawk. "I've been out here hiking with my crazy uncle since I was a kid. He said the natives talk about firebugs in the sky and shadow walkers haunting their people."

"Brah," said Emorie. "Are you serious right now?"

"Totally," assured Hawk. "They especially mention a portal to hell over by Kooakotch, a village just east of here."

"And you believe all that crap, Brah?" asked Emorie.

"Not sure, bro," said Hawk. "Even if it's not an actual portal to hell, there's always something behind weird stories like that."

"You mean like malt liquor and vodka?" said Willow.

"Hey, that's not cool," scolded Hawk. "It's their beliefs. Who are we to say they are crazy?"

"I never said they were crazy. Just drunk," said Willow.

Everyone laughed.

"Anyway dude," said Taylor, feeling a little bit jealous of Hawk's and Willow's exchange. "You should lay off the creeper material right now. I'm going to get some sleep and I'm feeling kinda scared right now," said Taylor.

"I wouldn't separate from the group," said Hawk. "They avoid strength and attack the weak when they are alone."

"They?" asked Taylor. "What, 'they'?"

"Shadow walkers," said Hawk as scarily as he could.

"I'd rather get attacked by shadow poppers then hear any more of your lame stories," said Willow.

"Yeah. I'm with Willow," said Sable as she lowered her now dry feet to her warm, waiting slippers.

Stab!

"Aaaaggghh!" cried Sable.

"What the heck, Sable," yelled Banks. "Quit freaking out!"

"Ow! Something attacked my foot!"

"It's a snake," yelled Banks.

Everyone pointed their flashlights and cellphones toward Sable's feet.

One of her feet was white and pretty, like a doll's foot, decorated with glittery pink nail polish.

The other was turning grey with black veins racing up her leg and black blood dripping from her petite toes.

She grabbed and clawed at it as the searing pain shot up the extremity.

"Help me you idiots, please," pleaded Sable.

"I don't see a snake, brah!" said Zaden.

They all started pointing their measly lights outward toward the darkness.

"Prrruiueeep!" was heard only a few feet away, but nothing was seen.

"What was that?" squealed Willow.

Out of a nervous habit, Zaden started picking his nose and eating his boogers.

"Aaagh. Disgusting!" said Taylor. "I thought you were high class," she yelled. "Garooossah!"

"Look!" yelled Rayden. "Oh, my God-uh. It's so cute," she said as she walked toward what looked like a cute little yellow puppy with large ears, rosy cheeks and a cute, puffy, little tail.

"Prrrjuuuiiieeep. Prrruuiiueep!" it squeaked.

"Oh ah! I want it," said Rayden as she bent over to pick it up like a little baby.

"My leg," moaned Sable with a weak, barely audible voice.

Then Zaden noticed a dot of bright red on the creature's fluffy tail. He realized it could have been Sable's blood.

"No Rayden!" yelled Zaden.

But Rayden was already holding the cute creature in her arms. Just then, it opened its mouth revealing a nasty mouth full of fangs and slime. It turned itself inside out revealing a horrible monster lurking inside. It attacked Rayden, going for the jugular.

"Help her!" yelled Sable with her last ounce of strength as she collapsed off of her cot onto the floor with an empty thud.

But everyone ran away as fast as they could. Hawk stopped and turned back as he realized he was running away. He immediately turned back toward the sound of Rayden's gurgling.

He grabbed a metal poker to attack the monster. But when he came upon Rayden, the creature was gone. Rayden had stopped making noises and was still, her eyes open in terror. Blood gushed from her neck. Hawk kneeled down by her side and grabbed her neck but he didn't know what else to do.

Piiuuurp!

He pivoted toward the sound but the creature attacked him from the side. But the thing was much larger now and was morphing into a full-sized chupacabra. Hawk fought, but it was futile.

"Aaaaagghhhh!" was heard by the rest of the group that had huddled together in the dark. The monster continued to rip Hawk apart. Its hunched shape was silhouetted as the fire still crackled. As it crunched bone and ripped muscle, the disgusting sounds could be heard by the huddled group.

"Hawk!" cried Taylor. Banks jumped on her and put his hand over her mouth.

"Shut up," whisper-yelled Banks. Taylor writhed and fought him as if he were a monster.

"Taylor," whispered Willow. "Please! I don't wanna die, girl."

Taylor relaxed. The group huddled on the cold ground behind a grass bush and looked toward the fire.

But it had been extinguished. It was silent once again. Everyone's heart was pounding beyond belief. They were sweating and panting. They heard claw marks skittering around them. They saw the red eyes. They were paralyzed. The scratching of claws grew louder as the thing got closer but kept popping up in different places to confuse the group.

Then, the sound stopped. They stared blindly into the darkness. All they could see was the giant hole in the sky filled with stars. The ring of storm clouds a horizon away was once again closing in.

The monster jumped and grabbed Bank's throat. Banks released Taylor. Taylor started screaming. Banks was being choked. He clicked his flashlight with his arms flailing about. The light hit the face of the chupacabra. Its face was about the size and shape of a horse head, except with long crooked daggers for teeth. Its slimy skin was smooth and white and had dark grey patches of fur. It opened its jaws and revealed how many and how large the spines of fangs it had. Slobber and saliva dripped from tooth to tooth and its hot, putrid breath smothered Bank's silent, tearing eyes.

The thing chomped down. It easily hunted the rest of the group, one by one. Alone. In the cold, wet eternal darkness. They were no more.

Stevens who was making her way south and east came upon a sparkle in the distance. She magnified on V-

VIDS. It was a green gemstone. She was confused. She got close enough to see it with her own eyes. She picked it up. It was a lone, beautiful, perfect, flawless diamond about the size of a small clear marble (a cleary).

"Where did this come from?" Stephanie asked out loud. Then she turned and saw a piece of broken gold. Her eyes kept moving in the same direction and then she saw the finger. She knew what had happened.

"No!" she cried. "I'm so sorry!"

"Stephanie!" called Hernandez.

"They were just a bunch of kids!" lamented Stevens. "How could I have let this happen!"

I looked at the count. Just like that, the green square had jumped from zero all the way up to eight. The first real casualties. Neutral. Innocent civilians.

All EEMO operators tapped into the feed to see the atrocity. They paused in silence.

"The fault is not yours, Estephanie," said the General. "There is only so much you can do. And right now, you have to know that we just saved many more lives. The other people who were out here. OA is moving more than 30 people out of the hot zone because of what we have accomplished so far. But we have to continue our work and finish what we started."

She was silent.

"Estephanie!" yelled the General. "Focoos. Remember your training."

She listened.

"Find that sucker," said the General.

"Yes, sir!" yelled Stevens. "I'm gonna waste that freakin…"

"No," said the General. "Bring it to me. I have special plans for it."

"What plans, sir?" asked Stevens.

"I do not know," said the General. "Not yet."

Stevens focused her resolve. She commenced a top-to-bottom scan of the area with the full array. She spotted infrared tracks in all directions but none led away from the location.

"I'm going to need a doggie," Stevens said over V-VIDS.

"Coming at you Ma'am," said Portman. He had already started his way north toward the group as soon as he heard the bad news.

"Right there is the last sign," said Stevens as she indicated the last known spot with lasers.

Portman's doggie started sniffing around.

"It's near, but I can't make it out," he said. His doggie looked up. "Nope. That's not possible," he whispered. He scanned all around and saw nothing. "Nope." Then he looked down. There was a spot at the very center that had no sign where there should have been something. Instead, it looked as if the sucker had brushed out. (A technique smugglers use to cover their tracks. They literally grab a handful of vegetation and brush away footprints from a dirt road or sandy patch to not be followed.) "That's the only way."

Portman's doggie started to dig furiously down into the moist, soft earth. Its giant paws clawed out buckets full of mud and dirt with every swipe. Then like a slimy worm covered in dirt, the killer sucker tried scurrying away into the darkness but Stevens spotted it. Portman's V-VIDS picked up the signal and pinned it down with its paws and under its claws. Portman launched a laser net at the sucker. In an instant, it was sucked up in the net and seal-wrapped up like a holiday ham.

"Bring it to me," said the General.

Instinctively, Portman absorbed the sucker into the doggie for transport. Normally, the minds of captives, civilians or even enemies are too weak to penetrate the onboard neural-magnetic isolation field generated by all EEMOs. But something had given the killer sucker unprecedented telepathic powers.

A supercharged jolt of electricity jarred every EEMO operator from the Babos to Quitobaquito. I felt like I had just been zapped by a Taser. Trust me it really hurts! The sucker had temporarily tapped into our neural network. But like a switch with too much juice, the fuse popped and prevented any damage.

"Gonzo!" called the General. "Cut him (Portman) off!"

"Already on it, sir," answered Cmdr. Gonzalez.

I surged toward Portman. Even though I had only been crawling for a few minutes, less than 10, it felt like an eternity. The damn desert goes on forever. No wonder so many people die out here. Exhausted, they reach the pinnacle of a mountain, hoping to see a road, a village or anything, but all they see are hundreds and hundreds of more pinnacles, extending all the way past the horizon. At that point, one would die of hopelessness alone.

Then, a million years later, I saw lights over a ridge, explosions. Portman's doggie was going bat-crap crazy! It was throwing gravity bombs, laser nets, plasma fire, magna-rockets, you name it. It clawed at the air. It bit nothing. It jumped and launched itself at solid rock, boring though solid peaks like a worm through an apple. It was destroying all the mountains in its vicinity. It was too volatile to approach.

"Gonzo!" I called.

"I know, Diamante!" grumbled Cmdr. Gonzalez in his own extra deep voice. "Stand by!"

I took cover behind a precipice. At Fortuna, Cmdr. Gonzalez finalized the controls.

"There," he said happily. "Take that!"

Portman's doggie dove forward and in mid-air went limp. It crashed toward the earth with a dead thump, headfirst into the earth, hind legs tumbling over the rest of the body. It came to rest, eyes closed.

In an instant, I was at Portman's doggie's side. It opened its mouth at Gonzo's command and Portman rolled out.

"Is the thing secure?" I asked.

"It's secure," said Gonzo, calmly. "He hacked the doggie but didn't know how to get out."

I jumped out of my scout and read Portman's vitals.

His heart was not beating. His brain activity blank; he had no signs of life. He was dead.

"DEFIBRILLATION VITAL," read V-VIDS. Along with a simple GIF of instructions.

I knelt by his side. Placed my hands in the correct positions and thought, "Zap!"

Portman's body jumped. Nothing.

"Zap! Come on, man!" I said. He grunted. His heart regained activity but it was very sporadic. His vitals lit up but then started jumping all over the charts. I was scared.

"Portman!" I yelled. "Portman. Come back bro!"

The doggie woke up and shook its head. Its angry eyes lit up again.

"What happened?" Portman asked softly.

"You're back, bro!" I said, wiping away my rebellious tears.

"Diamante," called the General. "Put Portman in the scout now! Gonzo will drone it back to Fortuna. You take the doggie and continue."

"Continue?" I yelled. Portman's eyes rolled back into his head and his head dropped. His vitals were active but unsteady. "Are you crazy? I need to make sure Portman is okay."

I focused back on Portman.

"Are you a doctor," asked the General.

"No," I admitted.

"Put Portman into the scout or else you are going to be responsible for his death!" threatened the General.

I pounded my fists into the earth in anger. I lifted Portman as the scout approached. He was scared too. "Hey!" I yelled. "You get better real soon! We're gonna see each other again. Real soon, you hear me," I reassured him. But I wasn't in his shoes. It was easy for me to be brave. The scout was in place and I placed Portman into its receiving jaws. I wondered if they were the jaws of life or the jaws of death. He reached out with his sweaty, dirty, bloody hand and gripped my hand super hard. I pressed as hard as I could.

"Real soon, buddy," I said.

He swallowed a dry gulp.

"Maybe in the next life," he whispered as his hand dropped down. His heart flatlined. The scout quickly absorbed Portman and jetted away.

"The doggie," yelled the General.

"The doggie?" I asked. "That thing is possessed. It killed Portman. I'm not getting into that..."

"Gonzo," called the General.

"It's back online, sir," said Gonzo. "With a patch."

"It's fine, Diamante," reassured the General. "I would never order you to do anything I would not do myself. Now, get in the doggie and bring me that sucker! I want it now!"

"Yes, sir," I said angrily. I made the switch. I got in the doggie and started settling in. It was still weird knowing the killer was still on board. The killer of Portman, the killer of all those hikers, the killer of who knows how many others. I didn't even know Portman's first name.

As I looked around his doggie, I saw that everything was orange blue and white. I saw white horses decorating random gizmos in the doggie.

"This guy's a die-hard Broncos fan," I thought. I checked V-VIDS. He was well on his way to Fortuna. Status 'Classified.' I thought that was strange. I thought over V-VIDS, "Real soon."

"Diamante!" yelled Gonzo. I snapped back to the mission.

"General, what's your 20?"

"Gunsight, south of 86," said the General. "The suckers are coming out of nowhere. I think I killed five near the village already."

"On my way, sir," I reported. I looked at my map and saw combat erupting everywhere. The blue friendly square now read one, presumably for Portman. From the looks of it, the forces were converging near the General. Of course, he was there, near the action, near the center.

"We're moving west,"' said Young. "We've cleaned house over here." He was in command of his own squad of Shadow Wolves, each with their own areas of assignment. His wolves reported only to him.

Hernandez didn't say anything but we saw she was moving east. She was too busy having fun killing. The suckers were no match for our tech. It was like playing a combat video game, with endless ammo, easy targets and you couldn't lose.

FILE 11 CHARLIE

The Ambush

"SOUTH?" called the General.

"We already crossed the line into Mexico, sir," said Hall. "We're approachin' Bonori and the rain is coming back at'cha." The thunder clouds that had been shocked outward were clapping back inward like water clapping around a plunging cannonball.

Hall, Turner and the AI scouts rushed forward into a wall of rain and lightning.

"There it is commander," said Turner, also calmly but with a certain intensity. "There's mad suckers scattering everywhere. Oh, I'm all about it, sir. I'm all about it."

On V-VIDS, the suckers were still raiding the tiny Mexican village. They could be seen dragging a family out of a little farmhouse. It was difficult to watch.

"Mike, take one of the scouts and head up around the range on the east side," said Hall. "Have the scout set up by the draw and you go high to the south. You'll be my sniper."

"Aye-aye, commander," said Turner. Just by that, I knew he was either a sailor or Marine. And either in or fresh out of the service. And with personal knowledge on how the Corps brainwashes us so deeply, that even decades after boot camp, I still replied to lawful commands with 'aye-aye' to Border Patrol supervisors until I got out of the habit.

"10-4, jarhead," chuckled Hall. "10-4, sir."

"Hoorah," laughed Turner.

Hall rushed forward, hugging the foot of the mountain that ran north by northwest, north of Banori. He set up north of the draw and sent the scout across and south but it stayed low.

I noticed the green square on V-VIDS had jumped up to 11. The system could only account for casualties that were confirmed and bonafide. But I knew the count was much higher.

"A'aight Mike, we ain't got no time, man. We gotta help these people now!" said Hall. "You just hang tight. We got NO idea what's waitin' for us up in here."

"Dangit! You're asking a lot of me, sir," said Turner. He felt like a thoroughbred, held back at the gate when all the other horses were storming ahead. "I'm in place, sir."

Hall's lion roared forward, swiping three suckers into ex-existence. His targeting system focused on a group of suckers and fired a spike bomb that ejects thousands of energy spikes in all directions, vaporizing anything within a 30-foot radius. The lion leapt again and bit another chupacabra in half.

Hall had brought a platoon of AI scouts in combat mode to supplement the fight. The AI scouts were lightning fast and dead cold in their precision. They were making quick work of the dozens of loose suckers. Hall ordered one of them to help him start clearing the little houses using life detection. The body count had already jumped by another five and Hall was trying to stop the losses.

The AI scout spotted more civilians in trouble. Hall fired a targeting round through the wall of the house and hit the stalking sucker. The scout started doing the same. Soon, with the help of all the other AI scouts, every house in Banori was cleared with no more casualties.

Hall's lion started prowling up the dirt streets of Banori. Only its bright green eyes and white fluorescent fangs glowed as the hiding villagers peeked out of their windows.

"Stay inside your homes!" announced Hall on a loudspeaker in perfect Spanish. The lion's mouth moved as Hall spoke. It looked like the lion was really speaking. "Do not come outside. We are handling the threats."

"Commander!" yelled Turner. "You got something big coming at you, from the east, sir!"

"What is it?" asked Hall as the lion kept announcing.

"Unknown, sir. It's cloaked. But whatever it is, it's big, fast and gunning your way!"

Hall faced east. Instinctively, the scouts in the village raced toward the threat even though they only saw an anomalous heat source. Half of the AI scouts were ordered to stay in the village. The deployed scouts fired their arsenals and hit the thing from different sides.

In the explosion, the cloak disappeared for a second, long enough to make out a giant chupacabra. It was about 25 feet tall and had four arms with sword-like claws. The scouts fired again and unleashed the full arsenal. The running sucker's cloak disappeared for good but kept going for Hall. The scouts leapt at the sucker's extremities and vital areas but the giant chupacabra swiped a handful of scouts away and grabbed another by the thorax. That scout bit the sucker with its mandibles and stung with its stinger but its defense was ineffective. The giant started smashing that AI scout on the ground.

Hall ran around the giant sucker and pounced from behind. The lion bit the thing on the trapezius muscle trying to get the neck.

"I see no other threats," said Turner as he raced down the hill toward Hall. "I'm going in!"

"Ahh. This thing is not going down," said Hall as he wrestled with the beast. The rest of the AI scouts covered the monster like a writhing, ruby robe. The lion's claws were ripping into the thing's hide, but the beast remained unfazed. The giant sucker kept smashing scouts and ripping them in half. The sucker then started reaching for Hall's lion. It stabbed the lion with its giant claws. One of the swords went through the flesh, narrowly missing the commander. The second group of scouts rushed forward and kept their distance but kept strategically firing at the beast.

"Cease fire, you stupid computers!" yelled Hall. "You gonna hit me!" The scouts stopped. Some looked confused.

Just then, dozens of more suckers popped up from the darkness in the desert and converged on Banori. The AI scouts in the village got to work, firing in all directions. Biting and stinging everything that moved, and keeping the invaders away from Hall.

The monster finally grabbed Hall's lion by the scruff and tried to smash the cat against a boulder but Hall leaped away to safety. He fired his entire array at the beast in a shower of fireworks, but it kept rushing forward. Hall fired all the weapons he had, but they were being repelled or neutralized by some sort of anti-offensive energy emanated by the giant. Refusing to get too close and make the same mistake twice, Hall evaded and struck with weapons at a distance like a sneaky boxer.

The beast was fast but not agile. It couldn't catch Hall. It was bleeding and breathing hard. It stopped and looked at Hall. It was trying to hack Hall's mind. And before he knew it, Hall was compromised. He froze. The monster attacked and grabbed Hall's lion and started mauling it.

"They always kill the brotha' first," muttered Hall. The beast drew three of its free arms back, aimed its claws right at Hall's body. But before the knives could make the kill, two of the arms were severed - one from each side - one top arm and one bottom. The beast made a hideous shriek. It was left lopsided and bloody.

"Not this time, commander!" yelled Turner.

The doggie was almost as big as the beast. Turner had fired a plasma-rang and it swooped back to the doggie. The scouts kept up their furious battle with the invaders, taking potshots at the beast when they could. One scout got dog-piled by dozens of suckers but kept fighting its way out. It was getting good accurate hits with minimal damage. The beast ignored the scouts. It then turned to the doggie. Hall remained motionless but his vitals were steady.

"He's okay," said Cmdr. Gonzalez. "Just make sure no one messes with him," he commanded the scouts.

"10-4," said the lead scout in a deep synth voice.

Turner saw the beast giving him the greasy eyeball.

"Bad choice," said Turner. He charged at the beast. The doggie's heavy feet thudded against the ground. The massive body hurled faster and faster. The beast gave a war cry and charged faster as well.

At the last second, Turner lowered his doggie's head and rammed the monster right in the sternum. Turner felt the monster's skeleton cracking underneath. The beast was hurled onto its back and lay there for a second as if its wind had been knocked out. Turner jumped on top of the stunned beast and bit off another arm at the shoulder. The beast got out from under the doggie and started running away, bright purple slime splattering all around.

"You didn't say please," said Turner. He fired the plasma-rang again and hit both legs. The stump of a beast fell and started flopping around. Its last arm scratching and stabbing at the ground. Turner walked up to the dying beast.

The lead AI scout pulled off the last remaining suckers, pestering Hall's downed lion. Hall came to. All enemies were either dead or dying.

"Commander, you're gonna wanna see this," said Turner.

"A'aight. I'm coming," said Hall as he shook off the beast's spell.

Turner fired a large laser net and shrink wrapped the beast.

"General," called Turner.

The AI scout helped Hall get back to his feet and both walked up to the bloody mess.

"Go," said the General, completely unimpressed by the battle. He knew other battles, just as dangerous, were still raging across the west desert. The friendly body count remained at one, but the neutrals had gone up by 15. The innocent farming villagers were the latest casualties. Even though they did their best, the team had failed once again to preserve all life. Still, Hall was okay. Thank God.

"What do you want me to do with this one?" asked Turner. You might want to see it, General."

"I already did," said the General. "I already have what I need. Take it out."

"Aye-Aye," grunted Turner.

Hall laughed a weak but healthy laugh. "Man. You still with that 'aye-aye' mess?" he chuckled.

"As you were," corrected Turner but instead made it worse.

"What?" asked Hall. Everyone on V-VIDS who was watching burst out into laughter.

"Come on Mike!" said Hall. "You not in the Corps anymore, man!"

"Hey!" chuckled the General. "Once a Marine, always a Marine, right Turner?"

"A-firm," said Turner. He turned to the beast. It was still trying to hack Turner.

"Ahh!" squealed Turner as if he had just seen the cutest thing ever. "Look at it. He's trying to hack my little brain," said Turner. Everyone kept laughing, but not clear if they were laughing with Turner or at him. "Nice try you stink bag!" He aimed the plasma-rang at the head. Hall and the AI scouts aimed in as well.

"So long..." said Turner then paused.

"Sucker!" said everyone and laughed out loud. The beast whimpered then, boom!

FILE 11 DELTA

Purgatory

UNDER the full spectrum of lights exploding across the sky from the battles and lightning, the Oaxacan who had been processed, deported and had made his way back to his area of operations, managed to slip past the first wave of Border Patrol agents and through the many surveillance nets.

The Oaxacan was leading a group of illegal aliens, mostly from Central AmVictora but he also held a married Chinese couple and two young Romanian girls about 16 and 19 years of age captives in his group.

His group was easily spotted by V-VIDS but the General reiterated his first order.

"Let Border Patrol and OA handle that," he growled. "It is not our mission. We must stick with the protocol."

Operators on V-VIDS groaned and hissed. But none dared speak. All kept fighting.

By now the rain had already smashed back onto the rez and the group of about 20 was soaked. They were using large, black plastic trash bags as ponchos but the rain was going right through anyway.

Bam! The Oaxacan fired an old rusty pistol in the group's direction. The women screamed and the men tried to console them.

"Andale! Hurry up! Move!" commanded the Oaxacan. Fear, threats and intimidation can be powerful forces. Strong enough to force people to do things they really do not want to do.

One of the young girls, Melina, would not move. Her sister Sasha begged her to move or else she feared the Oaxacan might do something hurtful to them.

"No Sasha," said Melina. "I did not travel across the ocean to be a slave! To be owned!" she shouted. Even though she was speaking in a foreign language, the Oaxacan knew enough. She was rebelling against him. He could tell she was no longer being controlled by fear, like the others. She was being guided not only by the spirit to survive, but by the indomitable spirit to fight. He had to crush her spirit so she could not embolden the others. The Oaxacan grabbed Melina by the hair and threw her to the ground.

"Oh," said the Oaxacan. "You want to laugh at me?"

Sasha reached out to help her sister but the Oaxacan kicked her to the ground as well. Even though he was only about 5 foot 4 and they were closer to 5-8, he was much more powerful with his dense, solid frame compared to their thin, lanky bodies that had been deprived of proper nourishment for weeks. Sasha tried to shake off the shock of the trauma but the Oaxacan kicked her down again. She let out a low moan of pain as she collapsed face down into the muddy ground.

"No!" shrieked an outraged and horrified Melina as she saw her older sister fall. The Oaxacan grabbed Melina by the hair and pointed toward Sasha.

"Anything you do, she will pay the price," said the Oaxacan. "Entiendes?" Even though Melina did not speak Spanish, some basic ideas are universally understood.

"Besides," said the Oaxacan as he softened his tone of voice. "I like you. You are my favorite. I can take good care of you," he said with a disgusting smile.

"Leave me alone! Just leave me alone you pig!" screamed Melina as she pulled her arm away. She reached back down to grab her sister up to her feet. Even though she knew she risked both their lives, Melina had never been one to obey. After all, that was partly why she was not safe at home, to begin with.

"Huh," scoffed the Oaxacan. "I'll get you later," complained the Oaxacan. "The rest of you animals, move! Anyone who falls back, I'm leaving behind for the chupacabra!" he laughed. He had already encountered the suckers on more than one occasion. Much like lions or cheetahs, the suckers generally only had to kill the slowest or weakest of the group so naturally, the Oaxacan was always spared.

When in the custody of the Border Patrol, the Oaxacan would melt into a puddle of sadness and pity. But out here, in the heart of darkness, in the absence of law or accountability, he ruled with impunity. He butt-stroked one of the Guatemalan males and kicked him in the butt just to show who was the boss.

The group was cold, hungry and exhausted from the nine days they had spent waiting to cross the line. So now, just hours into their illegal entry, they were near collapse.

During those nine days and nights, he had abused just about every person in unspeakable ways, building his terror and control over their minds and spirits. Had he not dominated them so forcefully, he feared they would have escaped by now. With some of the IAs paying or owing as much as $15,000 a head, he could not afford a single loss of one of his commodities. To him, they were not human. Only objects, only money, waiting to be paid. He was not human. He was worse than the chupacabra.

The Oaxacan drove the group across a flat dirt patch toward a wall of thickets. The group stopped at the edge of the wall. He pulled the heavy trigger of his rusty pistol again until it fired. The group dove head-first into the wall of thorns and stickers. Those who resisted were kicked in. Instantly they had to start crawling on their hands and knees. The mesquite bushes were so thick, the people literally could not stand up. Stickers and branches were scraping their palms, scalps, faces, chests and entire bodies as they moved. They had to fight through every inch of bush to progress. Far away, the Oaxacan saw lights approaching.

"Puta Madre!" he yelled. "They are coming for us, you idiots! Hurry! Get in there." Normally, he would have just hung out for an hour or two to make sure the group wasn't seen. But now, he had to push the group deep into an area he knew as El Manicomio or the insane asylum. Illegal aliens know it by that name because from ground level, you can't tell how expansive the thicket is. From the air, the maze continues for more than 20 miles of spines, thorns and misery, enough to drive anyone crazy. The Border Patrol knows it by a different name.

"Hey," said Agent McMasters, a horse patrol agent who was following the group. "Those crazy bastards are going right into Purgatory. Forget that. I'm not taking Honcho (his horse) in there."

"Keystone MSC," called McMasters. It was the Keystone MSC that had spotted the group in the first place.

"Yeah," called the grumpy operator.

"Can you keep an eye out for the group in case they come out somewhere's north?" asked McMasters as politely as he could.

"That's what I do," replied the grumpy operator.

McMasters and the other horse patrol Agents moved around into position. Sometimes the hardest part of being an Agent is the waiting.

"There's something else moving into Purgatory, right behind the group," called the grumpy operator.

"10-4," called McMaster. "Let us know when it comes out please."

"That's what I do," called the Grumpy Operator.

As the Oaxacan pushed the group deeper and deeper into the thicket, he sensed something else following them. He looked around and saw the flash of devilish-red eyes.

"Run!" he yelled at the group. He struggled through the thicket. He tried to push as fast as he could but it was nearly impossible. His face and hands were bleeding from the intense scrapes.

"Ahhh!" screamed a female from a distance. Others were whimpering and grunting, struggling to get away. There were two or three chupacabras hunting them with dozens more approaching. Their scrawny, wiry bodies were perfect for squeezing through the bush. As the suckers drew closer, the group pushed on through into a clearing about 200 feet across. They dove into the clearing and huddled together. The Oaxacan made it through right after.

"Forward, you idiots!" he commanded. "The chupacabra is going to kill all of you!" The group did not move. He put his finger on the trigger and forced the stingy trigger until it fired again toward the group. The bullet hit the muddy water and ricocheted away. They flinched but remained together. They had had enough.

The Oaxacan tried to imitate a monster eating a person but he only looked hystVictoral.

Melina stood up shivering and crying, not from fear, but rather from rage.

"You are not taking us," she said in her language.

"What?" said the Oaxacan. "What are you saying?"

"We would rather die than let you have us anymore," she said.

"Melina, no!" yelled Sasha.

The Oaxacan pointed his rusty revolver at Melina, 'La Traviesa' or the "trouble maker" as he dubbed her.

"Go ahead!" yelled Melina. "Do it!"

"I've had enough of you," he said with a scowl. He aimed the pistol at her. She stood bravely. But then he turned it to her sister. Melina's strong eyes changed.

"No!" she cried. "Please don't hurt my sister," she pleaded. This pleased the Oaxacan. He laughed at his triumph over Melina's will. But he did not lower the gun. He had to quell the rebellion.

The Oaxacan pulled on the trigger but it wouldn't move. He squeezed harder and harder but it had finally frozen from rust and dirt. He struggled with the weapon, yelling, smashing and cursing. But it became evident he would not be able to fire another round. Melina stood defiantly again as if it was her very will that had frozen the gun. Sasha urged her to back down. When the Oaxacan finally looked down at the old gun, a chupacabra silently stepped out of the thicket into the clearing behind him. It wiggled its claws and flashed its fangs as it prepared for the kill.

The group froze and just stared. They didn't dare warn the evil man that his demise was close. The Oaxacan kept messing with the gun. Another chupacabra crept out from behind the group, in front of the Oaxacan. He still didn't notice the second chupacabra walking past the mortified group and approaching the Oaxacan who finally jumped up when he saw it. The chupacabra swiped at the little man but the Oaxacan quickly dodged the attack and ran out of reach.

That chupacabra had managed to rip off the Oaxacan's coat, leaving him shirtless. His dark brown body was covered in evil tattoos including the Santisima Muerte, Malverde, skulls, skeletons, money, women, guns and other symbols of anarchy, power and destruction. He laughed at the chupacabra. He pointed the gun at the chupacabra and pulled the trigger again and it actually fired. The chupacabra teleported out of the way. The Oaxacan kept popping-off rounds until the gun ran out of ammo.

The group secretly smiled and looked at each other as if they had been saved by their very own demons.

A chupacabra crept behind the Oaxacan until it was breathing on his naked back. He stopped clicking. He turned around and looked the beast in its eyes. The sucker opened its jaws and raised its claws to slash and gnash. The group tightened their grip as they desperately held hands. It was all they could do.

The Oaxacan smiled and started laughing again. The group was confounded. Even the sucker seemed confused as it leaned its head and uttered a "brau?" Was this man who was at death's door happily going crazy?

The Oaxacan spoke.

"You think you can take me? You are in my home," he laughed. "I've been hunted by your family for years and I always get away." The suckers seemed to understand enough to be even more confused. His monologue gave the Oaxacan the chance to conjure the precious seconds he desperately needed.

The suckers, finally annoyed, decided they had had enough. But as their synapses finally fired the command to attack, the Oaxacan's eyes lit up with a dark, charcoal grey fire, yet black as evil. He motioned his hands in a "rise" fashion and out of the ground reached rotten bones, arms and fingers grabbing the suckers by their clammy limbs and tentacles.

The suckers' attention quickly turned downward, toward the death, rising. The Oaxacan paused, brought his legs and feet together, hung his head and stretched out his arms like a malevolent martyr. Two zombies busted through the earth at his side, handing him an AK-47 and a gold-plated pistol, encrusted in diamonds, emeralds and rubies. Both firearms were smothered in red mud and black blood.

"Take them with you my slaves!" commanded the Oaxacan as he pointed his guns at the aliens. His zombie slaves, the remnants of a rival cartel platoon, murdered in a mass grave, obeyed. Even though they had been murdered execution-style, their lifeless bodies moved like puppets at the whim of the Oaxacan and his dark magic. He owned their souls, even after death.

The zombie platoon attacked the suckers with machetes, throwing knives, hand grenades, small-arms fire and even RPGs (rocket-propelled grenades). The suckers tried to control the minds of the corpses but there was nothing to control; only gooey brains and dank skeletons wearing gaudy, gold chains and ostrich-skin boots. The zombies unleashed their assault.

The suckers were getting destroyed by subterranean zombies who were popping out of everywhere. The Oaxacan ran from cover to cover, ducking in and out as he aimed his death guns at the suckers. His combat prowess, sharpened and hardened in the cartel wars, was proving a force to reckon with. He feared no death. He was death.

In the fog of war, one of his zombies aimed his RPG at a sucker, but due to disrepair, instead of firing, the RPG exploded and blew the zombie up into thousands of putrid pieces. The rest of the zombie crew kept up the fight, undeterred by their comrade's demise.

The poor, bewildered group instinctively huddled together out of sheer fright. They had zombies on one side and blood-thirsty aliens on the other. With the suckers on the run, the Oaxacan turned his depraved gaze back at the group.

Black rays and mist emanated from his wicked eyes and from between the jagged spaces of his chipped teeth and depraved smile. His dark tattoos turned fluorescent and rearranged themselves into evil symbols like the pieces of a demonic puzzle upon the bloody, sun-burnt canvass that was his hide.

He threw down his guns and pulled out a straight razor — his torture weapon of choice. Its fierce edge glinted in the starlight and amid the rainy gusts of wind.

"He's glowing!" screamed a terrified boy from within the group. The Oaxacan aimed the daggers of his eyes upon Sasha and gripped his blade. He rushed at her to take a swipe. Black lightning shot out of his eyes as he lunged forward. The group closed their eyes, wishing only for a quick death.

But before the Oaxacan's blade slashed true, his body evaporated into pink mist. A dark spirit rose from the mist and jetted straight down to hell. The zombie platoon instantly collapsed.

Out of the shadows stepped forth Melina, the gypsy girl with blood on her face and a smoking RPG in her hands. But she could not pause for a breath. The suckers, now free from their own attackers, turned their aggression back toward the group.

"We belong to no one!" said Melina. "We were born free and we will die free," she said as she faced the remaining suckers. She dropped the empty RPG and picked up a red, burning stick.

"Maybe they will let us live!" yelled Sasha. But Melina knew it was over. She was at peace facing her death, as long as she went fighting. She knew the suckers did not care that she had just saved them from certain death.

The suckers kept approaching the sitting group. Another chupacabra entered the clearing. Then another and another. The young boy jumped up and darted toward the thicket but he was caught in a chupacabra's trance. The rest of the group stared in horror as a monster walked up to the young man. It pulled him into the darkness followed by several other monsters and they started feeding. The group yelled and screamed at the sounds of death.

The other chupacabras waved their clawed hands and opened their jaws to continue the feeding frenzy, but the nearest sucker was unexpectedly smashed to the ground by Hall's lion paw. Turner's doggie back-handed another chupacabra clear into the side of a rocky hill. Hall's lion slashed two other suckers with his razor-like claws. Turner bit another in half.

"I'm sorry, General," said Turner as he grabbed another sucker in his giant jaws. "I won't stand by and do nothing." A sucker tried teleporting away but Hall's lion fired a gravity ray at it, froze it and busted it apart.

"I'm with him, General," said Hall, killing another sucker. "Protocol or not, we're here to help, sir," said Hall.

"I see," said the General. "Do what you have to do. Then get your butts to Gunsight. They are all coming here."

"Roger!" said Turner as he and Hall made quick work of the remaining chupacabras.

Then, just like that, the monsters had been handled. Turner blasted a white laser-wire cluster at the heart of the thicket. The explosion cleared a smoking, burning path to the open desert.

"Is everyone okay?" asked Hall in Spanish. The group nodded yes. He and Turner led the group out of the thicket. The group of illegal aliens, some of which had come from half a world away, had traveled less than 1,000 feet into the Purgatory thicket. Had they remained in the endless labyrinth, most would have perished from madness, maybe all.

Even though they were breaking serious protocol by involving the Border Patrol, Hall and Turner called the group in. Once the kilo units were within eyesight, Hall ordered the group to sit. After what they had been through, Border Patrol custody was the safest place on Earth for them. They weren't going anywhere. Before the agents were on scene, Turner and Hall quickly disappeared.

"I got the group," said the grumpy MSC operator as if he had magically picked them up on his own. "Is anyone going to respond?" asked the grumpy operator.

"That's what we do!" quipped McMasters. Whistles, hoots and catcalls were heard on the radio as the other agents laughed and poked fun.

Turner and Hall looked down from the surrounding mountains as the red and blue lights approached the group. It was then that they realized that they would not be able to win the war without outside help.

"General," called Cmdr. Hall. "I think we might really have to break protocol, sir. "We are dealing with a lot more than we bargained for."

But the General would not listen.

"Negative!" yelled the General. "I called the right size of forces for this job. It is only a job. Everyone just do their job!"

Everyone remained silent; an awkward silence.

Soon enough, agents surrounded the group then transported them back to Papago Camp which was waiting with food, warmth and sleep.

FILE 11 ECHO

The Portal to Hell

"EVERYBODY," yelled the General. "They are coming to Gunsight!"

"Oh, heck no!" yelled Hernandez as an AI Doggie sped past her scout on the battlefield.

"Gonzo!" she yelled. "I want that doggie!"

"The one with the waggly tail?" answered Cmdr. Gonzalez.

"I'm gonna wag your butt all over the desert if I don't get that combat unit, commander!" yelled Hernandez.

"Ahh, ha, ha," laughed Gonzo. "Stand by," he snickered as he quickly reprogramed the doggie.

Hernandez ejected out of her scout, crossed her arms, made a sneer and started tapping her foot. Every second not in combat was agonizing to her. Finally, the AI doggie rushed forward and spun around into position.

"'Bout dog-gone time," shouted Hernandez as she ran toward and jumped at the doggie while it opened its jaws and took her into itself.

"And you're welcome, Ma'am," said Cmdr. Gonzalez in a sarcastic tone.

"General," called Hernandez. "We're all headed your way. What's your situation?"

"Teresa. I'm not 100 percent secure about Gunsight, but it looks like they are coming here from all different directions," said the General as he sounded like he was struggling. "They look like mutants," said the General.

"Mutants?" asked Hernandez and everyone else.

"Go underground Teresa," commanded the General. "You sneak in from below. The rest of you come ready to fight. Ahhh!"

Hernandez immediately dove headfirst into a cattle tank and started digging furiously. It seemed the doggie was almost as fast underground as it was above, especially in the wet, soft earth. All the rocks and boulders were left behind at the mountain ranges.

As I crested over the Gunsight hills, I started seeing the light show and heard the crackle of gunfire.

"General," called Young.

"Si, Quenton," answered the General as if he were still fighting.

"The Shadow Wolves are all reporting back-tracks to the 26 Hills, not Gunsight, sir," said Young.

"But they are all here, Quentin," rebutted the General.

"They are not there to stay," said Young. "They are passing through, sir. They are headed to the 26 Hills!" said Young in a frustrated voice. Even though he was not in charge of the operation, he was a great commander in his own right, not used to being second-guessed. The General shook his head in frustration. He did not like being wrong either.

"Are you sure, Quentin?" asked the stubborn General.

"Look at the sat picture!" said Cmdr. Young. "They're converging. If I had to say, they are gathering their forces. Whatever it is, it's happening at the 26 Hills right now!"

The General exhaled a grunt.

"Teresa," called the General.

"Copy, sir," said Hernandez. She had immediately diverted her course toward the 26 Hills. She knew he was wrong too but saved him the disgrace of having to utter the words.

She was skirting the east side of the GuVo mountains that led right to the target.

Then I saw the General's scorpion through the V-VIDS long-range vision. He was surrounded by mutant suckers. Big ones. Ugly ones with four arms and two legs. Their heads had grown to twice the normal size and their jaws resembled steel, bear traps. He was handling them but they were swarming him. I launched forward to fight at his side.

"Diamante," called the General.

"Almost there, sir," I reassured.

"I don't need you here," yelled the General. I couldn't help but feeling a bit insulted by his bluntness.

"Go to the 26 Hills. I and the drones will take care of these little guys. Heh, heh. Ahhh!"

"But, sir," I protested.

"That's an order! Don't bother me until I'm dead!" he commanded in his super-deep, fake-English voice. I flared my nose, furrowed my brow and tightly squeezed my lips together to keep my big mouth shut. He had a point. Hernandez was all alone and needed back up. Still, he didn't have to be so rude!

Meanwhile, Hernandez was approaching the 26 Hills from below the ground. She was steadily tunneling along until she hit rock. Her doggie slowed to almost a crawl.

"Come on you!" complained Hernandez. "I know you can do this. You got this!" Through V-VIDS was only darkness. Even though V-VIDS's sensors were developed to be powerful enough to look clear through the Himalayas, they were blank. Blind and unsure, Hernandez and her doggie struggled to break through the rocky foothills of the GuVo mountains.

The scraping and screeching of metal alloys against bare, solid rock were deep and high-pitched at the same time. Hernandez's body vibrated and the volume was like a trumpet blast directly into her eardrum. Then, with a last shriek of agony, the doggie stopped.

The experimental metals and materials unknown to the rest of humanity were proving to be no match against plain-old metamorphic and igneous rock.

Then, a chunk of rock about the size of a baseball popped off the rock face away from the doggie revealing a laser beam of white-orange light beaming at the doggie.

All of Hernandez's warning indicators went off at the same time. Extreme heat, radiation, magnetic fields, gravity warps and thousands of enemy proximity alerts.

"Chingao!" yelled Hernandez.

Her video feed instantly went live to all operators. Instinctively, as all heroes do, she went straight toward the danger and not away.

"Teresa!" yelled the General, as he struggled to fight his own demons.

"No puedo!" She warned the General to not even try the whole 'That's an order,' routine.

A lightning bolt blasted through the peephole and blasted a gap large enough for the doggie to jump through. Teresa leapt forward, into the flaming unknown. She landed on a giant, glowing boulder lining the inside of a fiery cavern rivaling Fortuna, only this one was burning and crawling with thousands of mutant chupacabras. She was not even one-tenth of the way down.

"The portal to hell!" yelled Young. "The elders were right," he gasped. Then he started speaking T.O. softly to himself.

"He's praying!" I said. "That's not a good sign!"

Teresa got her wits about her and went into stealth mode before she was noticed.

She crawled her doggie downward, toward the bottom, leaping from boulder to boulder.

"Teresa, get out of there," ordered Cmdr. Young. "Don't go down any deeper. You're not going to make it out!"

She completely ignored him. If she had listened to every man that had ever told her she couldn't do something she would have been stuck somewhere in some man's home, making tortillas and babies. There is nothing wrong with that. But she never would have been the hero she was meant to be.

As Hernandez descended deeper into the bowels of the fiery abyss the bubbling lava and the rumblings of the earth echoed in a cacophony of cataclysm. The extreme heat bent the electromagnetic spectrum into a blurry vision of intense light and flashed which made it almost impossible to see. She could only make out the whitish shapes of demons inside, crawling like bats on the inner-cliff walls. They flew in all directions with translucent fiery wings.

"Quentin, I need intel," she whispered.

"Our elders warned us of a portal to hell, Teresa. This is that portal!" whispered Quentin back at her as if she was already supposed to know what was going on. "The demons enchant with their beauty and power. We were warned never to go near the portal. It's a bad place, Teresa. It's filled with evil spirits and black magic. Remember Nino Quangi. Get out!"

"I loved Quangi," sighed Hernandez. "But I can't just walk away from my chance to make a difference, Quentin. You know that," said Hernandez. "You know I'm going to proceed with the mission regardless. So why don't you give me something I can use, cabron." She continued descending.

"Maybe," stumbled Quentin. "Maybe Quangi was wrong. Maybe the elders didn't understand what it was."

"Maybe that's exactly why I should be here."

"What?" whisper-yelled Quentin.

"Maybe Qyangi knew exactly what he was saying. It's we who didn't understand. He told me 'Don't fear your demons.' Maybe this is what he was talking about," said Hernandez. "All my life, whenever I ran from demons from one path, they'd be waiting for me at the next." A giant mutant landed next to her doggie as she continued down the furnace. "I always knew this day would come," she said solemnly.

"Teresa, give me some time," pleaded Quentin. "We can figure this out together."

Hernandez placed her finger over the 'Off' button to her stealth mode.

"Nooooo!" yelled the General.

"General!" I yelled.

"There's too many of them!" he yelled.

Luckily, I didn't really listen to his earlier command and I was still close enough to lend a paw. I turned around and jetted toward the General. When I got within visual range, I saw the General fighting like the Bruce Lee scorpion; felling suckers from all directions. His stinger flickered like the pulses of an electric strobe. His pincers ripped apart suckers at will. Still, they rushed at him like a tsunami.

"General," called Hernandez with a dire voice of doom. "I think. No. We underestimated them."

"No," denied the General. "We've been through worse."

"No," argued Hernandez. "Not like this."

"Teresa," called Cmdr. Young.

"I know," she said. "You were right, Quentin," she shook her head. "I hate it that you, out of all people are never freakin' wrong."

"No," protested Cmdr. Young. "That's what you like about me," he laughed.

"Shut up, Quentin," joked Hernandez, even as the certainty of her life faded by the second.

Hernandez stopped her descent; looked around. V-VIDS was practically jammed and scrambled. She was virtually blinded due to the high heat and light. She took in the situation. She was alone; in a portal to hell. She kept scanning for an exit.

V-VIDS gave out. All operators lost sight of Hernandez.

"Gonzo!" I called. "We lost commander Hernandez."

"Don't worry. I still got her," reassured Cmdr. Gonzalez. "I only got a blip but I can see her. She's climbing. Hold on... Dang it! We lost her." We gasped. "She's on her own."

"Negative!" yelled Turner. "We are going in!" but they were still minutes away. It might as well have been years.

Near the bottom of the abyss, Hernandez searched for a soft spot to penetrate and escape but the walls were covered in burning diamonds, crushed by the intense pressure and heat. They were impenetrable.

The demons appeared to have sensed a foreign presence and had blocked the entrance high above which was now her only exit. Her shaking finger still loomed near the off switch to the stealth mode. She faced a very difficult decision. She had to either turn off stealth in order to fight and risk a certain attack or stay unseen and eventually succumb to the fierce volcano.

"I'm not dying in here," she announced. She decided to escape.

"I got her," yelled Cmdr. Gonzalez. "She's still climbing back up to her initial entry point." He sent the coordinates to all operators so that they might help. Several nearby AI doggies and scouts blasted toward the entry point.

"ETA (estimated time of arrival) 60 seconds," said VL85, a.k.a. Vic, the nearest AI scout who was known for his person-like 'personality.' I thought about going as well, but the General needed my help.

"I'm not dying in here!" screamed Hernandez as she finally flipped off her stealth mode. "I'm fighting!"

Immediately, the beasts launched at Hernandez. And just like the General and the Bruce Lee scorpion, Hernandez began her own onslaught. She fired all of her weaponry at once, but her initial volley of traditional fire and explosive weapons was ineffective.

"Gonzo!" she yelled. "I need more firepower!"

"Sending experimentals now!" answered Cmdr. Gonzalez. In an instant, she fired a battery of quantum, freezing, vector vibrations and destructive ion streams.

The blast blew a tunnel through the demon bodies large enough for her to escape. She diverted power to her thrusters to cover as much ground as she could. The tunnel of mutant bodies collapsed around and behind her as she made her escape.

"I'm patching the new weapons array to everyone going in!" yelled Cmdr. Gonzalez. The AI doggies and scouts breached the entrance and started neutralizing demons.

"She's almost there!" yelled Cmdr. Gonzalez with excitement.

"I have visual. I see commander Hernandez," voiced Vic.

"Come on Teresa!" yelled Hall and Turner as they had almost reached the 26 Hills.

Hernandez looked up and saw Vic and the other AI scouts battling mutants, clearing the way to the cool, dark night sky above. That exit was her salvation. She bounded from boulder to boulder, zapping demons and striking in all directions. The AI EEMOs cleared the last of the demons so Hernandez could reach safety.

She gave one final push toward freedom. But a giant yellow hand, sparkling with fire and heat grabbed her doggie like a helpless ferret before it could escape.

The EEMOS immediately sacrificed their bodies, attacking the fiery fingers. The giant squeezed the doggie, crushing Hernandez inside. She grunted and struggled, determined to live.

With the help of Vic and the other AI fighters, Hernandez's doggie escaped the firey clutches once more and dove outside into the dark blue air burning comet's tail trailing behind her. Turner and Hall were in full sprint and could see the bright orange of the burning mountain.

Hernandez's glittering black eyes gazed up at the universe. She breathed freedom.

Just then, a green demon went in for the tackle. Her rising doggie, flung back down into the inferno. The giant fire monster once again crushed her body but she did not cry out.

"Grra!" she grunted and inadvertently let out a nervous giggle. "Dang, it! *Today* is the day," she whispered softly.

"Teresa!" cried Quentin, desperately flying full speed to her rescue. But he was too far. "We're with you!" he paused. "I'm with you."

"I know, baby," she smiled and grunted. Her black eyeliner started running down her face from the sweat and tears. Turner and Hall made it to the moth of the volcano but were swarmed by demons. They raged to fight through.

Again, she let out an involuntary giggle with a look of twisted agony and triumph. The beast squeezed the doggie. Her perfectly straight, gleaming white teeth started turning blood red. She forced her smile this time and concentrated her focus. Again she tried to free herself from the monster's grasp but it was futile. "Let me go, you... ahhh!"

The giant held up the doggie and looked in through its visor. Hernandez sat there and looked straight into the eyes of the beast.

"You got me," she smiled. "But I'm gonna get you back!" She convulsed in pain but then started laughing. She fired all of her weapons one last time at the beast's face. The blinded beast squeezed its fist.

A bright, white-blue flash exploded in slow motion within the burning inferno. True to her word, commander Teresa Hernandez, had faced the last of her demons. And now, for her, the secrets of the universe had finally been revealed.

When the blast had subsided, the beast was stunned. The bottom half of its body was wedged inside the fiery pit while the other half collapsed outside the crater.

Hall and Turner's EEMOs were flung, but otherwise unharmed.

"What did she do?" asked Turner.

"She set it free!" I said in horror.

"No!" argued Cmdr. Young. "She gave us a chance. She exposed it."

I wasn't quite sure. I stayed quiet.

"Gracias, Teresa," whispered the General.

I paused. We had just fought off the last of the General's attackers and survived. I had barely made it in time. But for Teresa, the war was over.

FILE 12 -

The King Rises

BEFORE I could think, I saw the demons escaping from hell at the 26 Hills. Whether they had been there of their own free will or against it, it didn't matter. They were out and fleeing by the scores.

Red and black lightning bolts blasted out from the crater in the side of the mountain. Fluorescent showers of lava, gasses and pyroclastic flows erupted from the crater. The giant lay there; glowing, pulsating, but still.

The scene was simply primordial. Like the very first spark of life on Earth, billions of lonely years ago in a tepid sea, or like the nearest bright horizon to mass extinction.

"Estephanie," called a calmer General.

"On my way, sir," answered Stevens, breathing heavily as she bounded, almost flying over the Diablo Mountains. "I'm sorry, sir. I'm almost there."

"Call Border Patrol," said the General.

"Border? Oh," said Stevens, full of surprise. "Y-yes, sir."

"Teresa was correct," said a somber General. "Hall, Turner, you were correct. Everyone was correct. I was wrong."

Just then, the highest peak on the 26 Hills blew its top with a massive explosion. Even though the General and

I were more than five miles away, we saw the bright flash instantaneously. But the shock wave was almost 30 seconds behind. We didn't wait for it.

The General, all the AI EEMOs and I shot straight for the blast wave and the 26 Hills with a war cry. We broke through the haboob that ensued and when we had made it through, we arrived at ground zero — the first ground zero of the day. When I got there I couldn't believe my eyes.

The explosion had left a crater about as wide as a football stadium, filled with a burning lake of bright, orange and yellow magma. I saw the escaping, vibrant-colored demons. They were long, shiny humanoids with smooth, leopard-printed skin. Some were red. Others blue, green, orange and even yellow. They exploded out of the lava lake, spreading their glowing wings and shooting straight up into the dawn sky. They dove back into the lava pool and rose back toward the sky again.

For a second, maybe an hour, there was no combat; no shooting or violence. We were in awe of the incredible sight. We only heard the sizzling waves of the lava lapping at the desert shore, the gurgling and popping bubbles and the fizzy splashes of the winged demons swimming in their fiery playground.

"Gonzo," said the General, almost in a trance. "Are you seeing this?"

"Yes, sir," said Gonzo quietly. "Is it real?"

"Call the dragons," ordered the General. "Call in everyone we have."

"Estephanie. Our friends?"

"They've been notified, sir," said Stevens. "They are on their way."

My eyes gazed east and my doggie's face felt the heat of the inferno. I saw the sky was turning yellow and pink, not from fire, but from the sun. Our battle was about to spill into the light of day. According to the plan, the war should have been over by now.

I felt blessed to have made it that far. I searched for a prayer, but all I could think of was, "Lord, light my way throughout this day..."

"Qu....nnn.tnn," said a staticky voice over V-VIDS. "Aaaar... uu theh...?" asked the specter of a voice.

"Teresa?" asked Quentin.

"Gennne...lll," asked the voice again.

"Teresa," said the excited General. "Is that you? Hernandez, we copy you. Go ahead!"

"This... What's the..." said the voice, preoccupied. It was Hernandez. It had to be. But how? "I'm not sure if you can copy, but the suckers mutated," said the broken voice. "I think they've been incubating in the volcano."

Everyone's lifted spirits dropped to the floor again. The transmission was in the past. It was the lost signal from Hernandez's time during the radio blackout.

"She's just now getting out," said Cmdr. Gonzalez. "It's from the past."

While Hernandez was deep in the hall of demons, she was gathering precious intel. She revealed the demons had developed a way to forge armor and weapons from the tremendous energy of the lava. The heat hadn't killed them as it would have killed any terrestrial being. Instead, it evolved them, creating unimagined bio-threats.

Many of the demons had tails like glowing, crystal morning stars like the blunt weaponry of medieval arsenals. Others spewed lava at will. Whatever powers they had amassed were like nothing before ever seen.

"There's something else," said the ghost of Hernandez. "I'm picking up traces of human DNA. There's a 99 percent match for with a former special ops..." the voice fell silent.

"The Mousey strain," thought the General to himself. But we all heard his thoughts loud and clear, as they pertained to the mission.

"What's the Mousey strain," asked Cmdr. Hall.

"It means deep in those demons' DNA, there is a trace of an old friend," said the General. Even though everyone wanted more details, the urgency was still on the battle.

"Where's the king?" asked Cmdr. Young in a frightened yet angry voice.

We were all scanning the area, looking for the king, a walking army. We spread out looking for any traces. Our EEMOs started sniffing the air and ground for chemical, molecular or even atomic traces of whatever had been there. Very quickly we realized we were not going to locate it. I don't have a lot of cool skills so I reverted to old school tracking.

I trotted my doggie to the last place we had the king. I noticed clumps of lava leading away from the fire lake. Even though there were pyroclastic rocks and chunks everywhere from the explosion, these seemed spaced out like something walking had left them behind. Then I noticed a giant, steaming rock that hadn't been there before.

"Commander," I said.

"Good job Mr. Diamante," said Cmdr. Young. "You sure you're not a Shadow Wolf?" he said with a grin. I smiled.

"I'm sure about that, sir. But I'm not sure what I found," I said. The giant igneous boulder didn't move. The flying demons started to circle around it. The demons were so mesmerizing to watch. They were beautiful but evil. Majestic, but revolting.

The boulder remained, but I noticed molten, hair-line fractures spider-webbing out around its circumference. It was about to hatch. The fractures continued to split until the rocky boulder crumbled apart and revealed the sleeping giant within. The monster uncurled itself from a kneeling, fetal position and stood in all its horrendous glory.

It stood about 50 to 75 feet tall. It had a head like a Great Dane, teeth like a T-Rex, long, sharp silver alien eyes, the body of a gladiator, four giant clawed arms and two muscular legs. But it wasn't glowing anymore. It wasn't an energy being. It was just a giant ugly beast.

The demon looked around, assessing the enemy forces as if it had its own V-VIDS technology. The flying demons landed and all knelt before the giant demon which at that point, we figured out who he really was.

"All hail the king," said the General.

"The chupacabra king," I added.

He must have heard us because he immediately scooped up four giant handfuls of lava and stones and hurled them in our direction. The fire rocks flew at us like a red sparkling comet until exploding at the ground before us. We all jumped out of the way, avoiding being almost cooked alive.

At the same time, scores of regular chupacabras were descending upon the 26 Hills from all over the West Desert.

"Estephanie!" yelled the General. "Where is Border Patrol?"

Just then, I saw dozens of vehicles, motorcycles, ATVs, Kilos, Jeeps, Hummers, horses, sand rails, razors,

Blackhawks, A-Stars, UAVS and even agents on foot. Usually, BP vehicles are not equipped with assault weapons. But these vehicles and Agents were armed in full battle rattle.

Ecstatic Border Patrol Agents who had joined the fight were gleefully engaging the endless droves of suckers. After hours and weeks and years of watching the fence rust, in the middle of the middle of nowhere, they finally felt that their time to truly defend the border and the country had finally come. The king pointed toward us and his flying slaves took to the sky, ready to either kill us or die trying.

Meanwhile, in Sells, there was a little, blind viejita (old woman) setting up her tamale stand for the day. She heard a rustle of noise behind her. She figured it was an early customer.

"Come here, mijo. Do you want to buy some tamales?" she said in her sweetest voice. But the customer turned out to be a deformed, retarded and lost chupacabra that was looking to eat the viejita, not the tamales. It snorted and grunted as it grabbed her by the arm. It would have just hypnotized her but it was too stupid.

"Ay cabron!" yelled the viejita. Not only had she already been robbed before, but she had encountered suckers before and lived to tell the tale, but no one had ever believed her. This time, she was ready with a little .22 pistol tucked under her large, saggy bra.

She quickly pulled it out and with golden teeth, silver hair and grey-washed eyes, she fired several shots. Like the amazing Sonoran bat, she had developed super hearing. She had learned to amplify her auditory senses due to her lack of sight. Two of her shots closely missed, but a single bullet hit the sucker right between the eyes. The bullet entered the skull but didn't go through. Rather it penetrated the alien skull and bounced around, ripping apart the sucker's brains.

The creature fell before her, chittering and sputtering blood. The viejita kicked it in the side and pushed it over into a running wash. Before she realized it, she was trying to stop the thing from falling into the water. Again she had survived and again, no one would believe her.

"Oh well," she shrugged her bent old shoulders. "Tamales! Tamales!" she continued on with her day of work.

Back at the 26 Hills, Cmdr. Gonzalez had patched Border Patrol over to the comms (communication) link portion of V-VIDS so they would have comms access, albeit limited and compartmentalized.

The General felt he was losing control of the situation and finally decided to summon whatever military units were available. Luckily, the 10th Mountain Division and 101st Airborne Divisions at YPG were gracious enough to help. Air Force units moved in from the north and east from BMGR and DMAFB. Together, they brought enough land and air power to wage a small-scale.

The units came in with heavy machine guns, GAUs, attack helicopters, warthogs and infantry paratroopers. The warfighting immediately erupted. Because of their powerful, yet traditional explosives-based weaponry, these units were given the designator of Fire.

The GAUs and attack helicopters' machine guns lit up and sounded like 500 drum rolls battering off all at once. The tracer rounds ripped through the 5, 10 and 20-foot tall suckers attacking below. The glowing red tracers looked like a thousand red marbles bouncing and skipping across the valley floor and into the clouds.

The air units also had to try and protect the infrastructure which the suckers were destroying. My thought was that they didn't know what the towers were for, but they knew they were important to us. Without the towers, every other agency would be fighting blind and with no comms. Although it did help contain the integrity of the mission which at this point I feared would be compromised very soon.

The Fire units set up fields of fire targeting the suckers on the ground. Most were approaching the King from the flanks, so the fire units dug in. The King started moving north to the doom of any unit in his way. He immediately teleported, leaving a swirling vortex of rain and smoke behind him.

The king emerged where the desert meets FR-1 (Federal Route-1). FR-1 led straight south toward GuVo, one of the most populated villages on the rez. The road continued on toward PiaOik and Menengers, other heavily populated villages, currently out of the kill zone and currently relatively safe. But if the monsters made it south, their people surely would not survive.

In the kill zone, as A-10s swooped at it with heavy firepower, the king uprooted a giant, steel electrical pole as tall as his own body. He ripped it out of the ground, cement footing and all and yanked on the power lines. The pole fit perfectly in his gnarly hand. As he pulled it away, he ripped with it high-tension wires, transformer boxes and electrical components.

The mess exploded into showers of electrical sparks and spread both ways along the electrical lines. The zapping, blue bolts of electricity crackled around the wires as the king began to use the pole and wires as a giant whip. The steel whip instantly swatted a jet fighter out of the sky like a common housefly.

The entire rez lost power. Not that there was much of a difference anyway. They already lived like people from the old west or a third-world country. They never would have imagined it would be an advantage to be so low tech. Luckily, there was little impact on the people so far.

The king quickly teleported back toward the fire units, swiping away dozens of warriors with a great arc of explosions as his whip struck military vehicles and personnel. The Fire units unleashed a storm of bullets and lead on the monster. Unfazed, he hurled rocks and ripped people apart like insects. Tiny warriors charged at him with M-4s and bayonets, slashing and shooting at his stumps of legs. They drew fluorescent blue blood but they might as well have been mosquitoes.

The military units continued to infiltrate the area with parachuting tanks, LAVs, hardened Hummers and ground fighters.

"Fire in the hole!" yelled Lt. Col. Havoc, an old crusty combat officer in charge of the arriving military units as he fired an RPG as he plummeted down in his parachute.

"Gracias amigo," said the General

"I ain't your amigo, amigo," said Havoc in his rusty, crusty angry voice. "I'm only here on orders and so are my men," he added on his military walkie talkie.

"Same old Havoc," laughed the General. "Amigo, you know what to do."

"Stay out of my way and I'll stay out of yours," barked Havoc.

"Muy bien, amigo," said the General.

"I ain't your dam amigo, you…" said Havoc before an explosion muffled out his extreme views on other cultures.

Havoc's units set up a perimeter but it was quickly engaged by the king's flying legion. The demons swooped down, slashing the Fire units with their morning stars and lava streams, erasing any combatants in their path. The friendly body count was rising sickeningly fast. The Fire units fired back but the demons were hard to hit from the ground.

Even though the General knew Havoc was a difficult man, he knew Havoc was honorable at the core and it was hard to watch his men die.

Havoc quickly redirected his might toward the king but it only opened his forces up to attack from the demons. Machine gunners scrambled to find natural craters, crevices, hills and washes for cover. It would give them a better chance to reignite their attack.

Helicopter miniguns spewed bullets like a water hose spraying droplets of water over the scene. The combat jets were engaging from afar but with such close combat, they had to engage from a closer distance. The demons did not waste time revising their strategy. Most would stay in the ground fight but several others sneaked up high and engaged the passing jets.

Havoc's forces were getting wiped out. I started to lose hope.

Just then, I detected a dark speck forming in the eastern sky. It loomed; black and glittering like a dark star. It then split into three separate shards, then seven. Those then started rotating in the sky around each other in a perfect, spinning circle.

The seven shards kept approaching and kept growing larger. Only at the last minute did the shards burst apart into seven swarms. The war raged on and no one but me seemed to notice. The swarm swirled into itself and blended into a black wave, washing around the sky like a plague of locusts.

"Is anyone seeing this?" I asked. No one responded. The swarm grew larger and drew closer.

"Stand down, Diamante," said Cmdr. Gonzalez as he saw my weapons array start their targeting sequence. I waited. Then I saw on V-VIDS the swarm was made of war dragons. Finally, we might be able to get the upper hand with a little death from above.

The incoming dragons had all been upgraded with all the experimental weapons inspired by Hernandez. As the dragons flew in, Cmdr. Gonzalez patched in the new suite of weapons to all capable EEMOs in the field. Every unit with the new capabilities was designated Expo.

The swarm descended upon the demons like a plague. Their robotic courage was terrifying. The dragons effortlessly zipped in and out of the flying fire, bullets and ordnance like they were dancing on a pond. The first wave of dragons plucked demons out of the sky by their wings and feasted upon their fiery bodies.

But the demons fought back. They started joining forces in twos and threes and fours. They linked up and created a sort of bio mesh to ensnare the dragons at their own game.

A red demon dug its hind claws into a dragon's visor then raised its clawed hands. The hands glowed white-orange with heat, then it plunged them both into the visor. The demon crawled inside and ripped the dragon apart from the inside, quickly killing it. All the while, the dragon was plummeting to the Earth and both died in a fiery explosion upon impact.

But the expo units' new weapons array was causing much more damage. They were atom-freezing the beautiful, horrible demons in midflight, sending them to their deaths below. The demons were rendered useless due to their inability to catch or match the speed and agility of the dragons. They were being slaughtered.

"Don't let up now," ordered Havoc. His team was on a roll against the suckers. "I want you to smash every last one of those maggots until they are all gone."

"Yes, sir!" replied the handful of human pilots. The rest of the AI dragons did as they were told. Most of the dragons, as with most of the entire friendly forces were AI but were savage learners. They continued to emulate the instinct, prowess and cunning of the handful of real, human operators.

The dragons continued the battle, employing swarm warfare. When a demon attacked a dragon, a hole in the swarm opened up leaving an empty space, leaving the attacker vulnerable from behind.

A single dragon broke away from the swarm and headed straight for the king. The demons, focused on the swarm, missed the single dragon. It fired all the weaponry it could right at the King's giant ugly head.

When the barrage smacked the back of the King's fat head, it stumbled forward before turning around to target the offender. But by the time the king had spotted the target and fired a ray of unknown composition the dragon operator was far enough to zip and flip harmlessly out of the way. The pilot had to be human. No known AI would ever break ranks in such a manner. At least not yet.

"Who's in command of that dragon?" yelled Cmdr. Hall.

"Vic?" I asked.

"Vic was killed in the portal," answered Hall.

"It's Portman, sir," he said with an audible grin.

In my mind, I could already see his gap-teeth, shiny, tan, bald head and leathery smile.

"You said real soon but I did think it would be this soon. Heh, heh, heh," chuckled Portman.

I quickly patched into V-VIDS to get a look at him. But when I got visual. He wasn't there. I only saw an orb of glowing light at the helm. It was an avatar.

"Maybe we can be born again," laughed Portman.

The King erupted in anger from Portman's attack. He directed his gang of demons to attack Portman. The demons disengaged the dragons and shot after Portman.

"Aaight Portman," said Hall as he took command. "You got their attention now. Let's use it against them. Hook back up wit' the swarm and y'all head north of 86. This is our only chance of splitting them up right now."

"Si. Very good commander," said the General. "We can dominate them on our conditions. Commander Hall, don't stop until you get to Burro Gap."

Hall's lion sprung across the landscape, keeping pace with the flying creatures.

"I'm on it!" called Hall.

"Alright boys," snarled Havoc. "Give 'em hell!"

The soldiers prepared to once again fire upon the retreating demons.

"Do not engage!" yelled Hall. "I say again. Do not engage those demons." Havoc remained silent as did the Fire units. The dragons continued north, feigning a retreat.

"Now what in tarnation do you think you're doin'?" yelled Havoc.

"Colonel, we have to break up the forces, then we attack once they are separated," instructed Hall.

The dragons kept flying and maneuvering as if they were running scared for their lives.

"Go ahead. Keep hauling," said Hall. "They'll probably punk out as soon as y'all hit'em up."

"Heh heh heh," chuckled Portman. "I'm all charged up and ready to rock, sir. You just tell me when to drop the hammer."

"Aaight Portman. That's good to know, sir," said Hall in his calm voice.

"Oooh, I'm ready to go, sir!" said Portman, trying to contain his enthusiasm.

"Aaight, now. We tryin' to keep you on the team a little longer this time okay?" chuckled Hall. "I'm gonna go with you."

Very quickly, the sky cleared of flying things and even rain. The King was left with his own swarm of suckers and a war to fight.

"Now may I please fight my war?" asked Havoc sarcastically.

"Colonel," said the General. "If your boys want to fight, this is your time."

"If you're scared, say you're scared," joked Havoc.

Havoc's men tickled their triggers in anticipation. A cool, moist desert breeze blew by.

The suckers and the King were eerily still, licking their chops.

"Fire at will! Fire at will!" bellowed Havoc.

Bullets, mortars and rockets started mowing down the suckers. This agitated the suckers and reignited the battle. The King seemed unfazed.

"Get some!" said Havoc.

A dirty, stinky wave of flesh, hair, claws and teeth rushed at the Fire forces. Havoc's men spewed fire but the wave overwhelmed them in places. Some soldiers were down to hand to hand combat. Up to that point, the suckers' mental trickery had been negated, but I didn't know why.

I personally was fighting alongside a soldier who had been ejected from her vehicle so I ran over to help her. I picked her up with my doggie paw and started reading her vitals. V-VIDS saw that her vitals were not in any real danger, but picked up on unusual brain activity that resembled something I had seen in an EEMO's 'brain' activity.

I shot a blast of pure oxygen at the soldier's face and she woke up. She looked confused and scared.

"Hey Ma'am," I said while projecting my face through the EEMO so she could see that I was human. "You're going to be okay," I said with a smile. But it wasn't the EEMO that was bothering her.

"Who are we?" she asked me, then broke out in a hystVictoral cry. "Why are we here?" she continued.

I opened my mouth to find words. But before I could even breathe a sound, she snapped back into combat mode.

"Get some!" she yelled and jumped off my paw and ran straight back into battle.

I was utterly confused. I turned my head and saw Havoc standing there with a contraption in his hand and an ugly smile on his face.

"We're burning daylight!" yelled Havoc at his people while he still stared at me. "I wanna wrap this thing up by chow," he yelled as he too jumped right back in the fight. Whoever or whatever he was, he led from the front and I had to respect him for that. But something was not right.

"Oh well. No time for that," I thought.

The General bit his lip. He was not comfortable with Havoc taking charge but after all, they were Havoc's men and he was winning.

Even though the suckers were losing, more and more of them gained the ability to take over the minds of more soldiers. It was weird. The soldiers would be in full combat mode and then all of a sudden, they would drop their weapons and start freaking out on the ground as if they were in great misery. The suckers would then move in for the kill.

Up north, the dragons had reached Burro Gap. The demons were in pursuit when the dragons swooped down into the hills. Hall instructed them to hide as best they could and use the rocks for cover.

"Alright," said Hall. "As soon as you get the chance, make your move. But don't kill them!"

"What?" asked Portman. "That's the only reason I'm here. They kinda owe me one," he cleared his throat. "Sir," he added.

"You remember Portman," warned Hall. "This is your last shot. After this, we can't bring you back at all."

"I've already been to the other side, sir," rebutted Portman. "I'm ready to go back."

"Okay. Try not to kill them. At least not all of them," corrected Hall.

"So you want us to kill or not," asked Turner.

"Win the battle and put your safety first. But I'm betting the King might want to save whatever family he has left. You feel me?" asked Hall.

"Roger," said Turner, Portman and the other operators.

FILE 13-

The Play

IT was a simple play. Nothing revolutionary or sneaky like trick plays in football. Hall figured if enough demons were injured, their suffering might summon the King to them. This would give us time to reduce the number of demons and get the King north of 86 for our final move.

When you are in a dragon, facing down a demon, you're not able to think about how to injure it enough to incapacitate it, but at the same time leave it with enough life to cry out for help.

Just like our training, we only had time enough to think about stopping the threat. If we played around with trying to shoot someone in the leg or arm, we could miss and be killed ourselves. Or perhaps worse, miss and kill an innocent civilian.

So as it played out, most dragon operators were fighting to survive. Luckily our problem was being too good of killers. We were losing dragons here and there but for the most part, we were still getting the better of the fight.

Stevens, who had acquired a dragon, had her eyes on a demon gliding below her. It was bright red and its glossy skin glistened in the sun. The tan desert and rocks passed by as the demon searched for its next target. It fired a stream of ionized gas at a dragon but missed. Stevens folded in her wings and dove in like an Olympic diver, sleek and quiet. She was determined not to let the demon strike again. As she dove she reached bullet-like speed.

Steven's dragon punched the demon in the back like an old truck engine, not from weight but from the sheer momentum. From behind, the demons were not as deadly. As they plummeted, Stevens grabbed the demon's wings with her claws and held it in place with the spurs on her legs. The demon squirmed and struggled to escape but Steven's was not done with it yet. She got goosebumps out of disgust from feeling the monster's hot body wrestling to save its own life. Once the wings were clipped she curved out near the bottom of her descent and flung the creature at an angle toward a thicket as to not kill it. Its body smashed into the mesquite trees and it struggled to get up but it wasn't dead.

Steven's silently zoomed straight up and away.

"That's how you do it!" yelled Hall.

"Mmm," grumbled Stevens.

"Nice job Stephanie," praised Hall.

"Not really. But thanks," countered Stevens.

The close proximity was necessary to the plan, but it was also easier for the demons to get a hold of the dragons. The demons started getting the chance to use their own array of strange weapons. Some dragon operators were not trying to save anything. They were just killing and no one could blame them as the demons were doing the same. But the AI dragons were better at controlling their impulses and were creating more casualties.

"General!" called Hall. "How's our boy doing?"

"We haven't seen the General," said Young. He's bypassing V-VIDS. But the king is not impressed. I'm not even sure he shares a connection with the demons. We might need to rethink the play."

"Turn around Sean," said the General in a creepy strange voice. Cmdr. Hall turned around and saw the General holding a sucker by the throat with his pincers. "Remember this one?"

Hall remained silent and puzzled.

"Organ Pipe," lamented Stevens.

"I'm going to present him to the misery mechanism," said the General.

No one knew what that was.

"It's telepathic breaking and entering," said Cmdr Gonzalez. "Quickly followed by threats, intimidation, torture, assault and battery and finally, psychological decapitation. We developed it from their own mental torture techniques."

"May I pull the trigger?" asked Stevens in a dead-serious tone. The General nodded and a red button appeared in front of Stevens. Tears welled up and her blue eyes flushed pink and sad. "They were just kids. Innocent kids you bastard," she said as she slammed the button.

The sucker instantly jolted and convulsed as if it was being shocked by 2,000 volts of electric chair power. We waited, and waited. It kept jolting and rolling in the dirt. But it wouldn't die. It was subjected to limitless agony and horror.

Some of the men began getting uncomfortable. The General kept his mad smile and wild eyes.

"General," said Portman. The General was silent. "Sir, this is cruel and unusual. We're better than this and it's against our Constitution!"

"Fry the bastard," countered Stevens. "You didn't see what this thing did to those kids or what it still hasn't done to their families. Fry it. Fry it 1,000 times!"

"Commander Young," said the General. "Do we have the King's attention?"

"Yes, sir!" answered Young. "He's stopped attacking and seems very confused."

"Here," said Turner as he threw another wingless demon at the General's feet. "Fry this one too." The body flopped down on the ground and the General zapped that one as well.

The chupacabra King let out a bone-shaking roar and all the other suckers instantly started teleporting toward Burro Gap. The King waved one last swipe with his whip, sadly killing more men before he too disappeared.

As the suckers started arriving at Burro Gap they desperately attacked everything in sight, trying to help their kin. Within a few minutes, almost every single sucker and demon was within less than a two-mile radius. The fighting was ferocious as both sides simultaneously had the best and worst conditions imaginable. But the King was nowhere in sight.

The General grabbed another fallen demon and zapped it as well. Just then, his scorpion was hurtled toward a steep, sheer rock face. He oriented in the air and hit the giant boulder perfectly with his legs and feet absorbing the impact. He looked back and saw the King holding his loyal but dead subjects in three of his hands and his whip in the other. The King was mad with anger and grief. This made the General very happy.

"Looking for me?" said the General. He fired the misery mechanism at the King and the King dropped. But the General quickly realized he wasn't going to be able to hold him for very long. "Brraa! He's too powerful," grunted the General. He gasped for air and was short of breath. His vitals were going haywire. He started sweating bullets and grinding his teeth.

"Havoc!" called the General.

"I told you," snarled Havoc. "I got things under control down here. The people are safe and I'm wiping the floor with the last demons and suckers still dug in the lair. I'll dig a mine straight to hell if I need to." He paused. "I'll take care of everything over here… amigo. Out!"

The General collapsed in his scorpion and the EEMO froze. The King stirred, then rose to his feet. He aimed all four of his hands at the General, inflicting his own organic version of the psychological assault.

"UUgh!" grunted the General. "Not yet!" He pulled himself together. Literally any other human on the planet would have instantly died. But the General's own anguish and battle-scarred soul was a hardened wall protecting his life.

"Hall," called the General.

"We got these guys, sir," said Cmdr. Hall. "Only you can dethrone that King." Since Hall had basically already been in charge of three battalions, his transition to temporary full command was seamless. It was as if the General had been holding back in order to prepare his commanders for their own time to lead.

The General launched forward and attacked the King who was easily 50 times the scorpion's mass. But as in real life, a scorpion can attack and even kill a much larger opponent. The General's stinger injected radioactive venom that started decaying the King's muscles. But the King bit off the scorpion's tail and spit it back at the General, making a fiery explosion and leaving a green glowing goo all over the scorpion. The General pinched off several of the King's fingers, forcing him to drop the scorpion.

In the background, Hall and the Expo force were swimming deep in the waters of war with no shore in sight. I saw a chance to help the General and attacked the King from behind and bit the scruff of his neck. I ripped out a chunk of rotting meat from its neck and went in for more but the King grabbed my doggie. Before he could do real damage, the General scurried back into the King's kill zone and plunged one of his pincers into the King's eye.

The King flung my doggie and me but we were not seriously hurt.

"Diamante!" yelled the King. "Help the others. I'll take care of this cabron!"

I saw Portman and Turner battling their own monster, another 25-foot version of one of the King's guards. It was about 1000 yards from the King and was fighting every inch back toward the King. "We can't let it make its way back toward the King and General," said Portman.

"I need half a mile," said the General.

"Why?" I protested.

"You need to help us now Diamante!" commanded Hall and he swooped in and started clearing the area of the General's request. I had to act and help out with the plan I didn't understand. Good soldiers follow orders.

We fired, froze, zapped and shot our enemies clear of the clear zone. As soon as the area was clear, I looked back toward the General. I felt like I was going to be turned into a pillar of salt for doing so. Quietly, unannounced and without fanfare, the General erupted a time bubble, sealing himself in with the King; both sealed away from the world and the world from them.

We continued fighting until the sun was high in the sky. We had been fighting for about 16 hours straight but we were nearing the end. The monsters were close to being all wiped out. Havoc's air units had even joined the Expo force to clean up the last of the suckers. His ground units had destroyed or trapped any remaining suckers at the 26 Hills. Their mission was accomplished. We were about to complete ours but the General and the King were still trapped in time and space and we knew nothing of their fates.

A few of us made our way back toward the time bubble and saw no signs of life or any activity. Then as if the General had been waiting, the bubble opened up and he had one of his feet on the King's bloody and battered head.

The King was limp and unconscious and near death but it was still alive. The scorpion too was heavily damaged and corroded. The General's skin was grey and his eyes completely bloodshot red. He smiled and showed his blood-stained teeth.

"I can't kill him," he laughed, then coughed a deep hoarse cough. "He's too strong."

"General," pleaded Hall. "You've got radiation poisoning, sir. We need to get you treated immediately."

The General smiled and shook his head.

"Stevens, Turner, contain the King," ordered Hall. "We'll kill him later. Diamante, help me get the General."

"Negative," said the General. "I have to do this myself."

"No you don't, sir," argued Hall. "We can help you."

"This is a gift. Don't you see?" said the General.

"A gift?" argued Hall. "Are you crazy, Hector?"

"I've wasted so many days," spoke the General. "So many days — wasted," said the General. I didn't know what he was talking about. The others? Maybe. "My entire life has been a misery mechanism. This is my chance to make one last difference my way, like Teresa."

"Don't you say her name," argued Hall. "She didn't want to die. She fought to live; for all of us."

"She was my friend too," said the General. "The Chupacabra King took her from us. I have to make sure he doesn't take anyone ever again. I need to make sure this is finished once and for all. It's been going on for too long."

The weakened Chupacabra King made a guttural roar as if he was summoning help. But there was no one left to help him, to the best of our knowledge.

"Young!" called the General. "You know what to do after."

"Yes, sir," said Young, who had been missing for quite some time. "I knew Teresa better than anyone, Hector. She wouldn't want this. Believe me."

"It ends now," said the General.

"Adios," whispered Young for the second time that day.

"Wait! No!" we protested.

The time bubble flashed and a bright light erupted within and without. The intense light and heat slapped our faces and we were forced to turn away; away from the explosion, away from destruction, away from the General and away from his choice. I honestly believed the General had ignited a nuclear explosion within the time bubble. Maybe he did. The world will never know.

FILE 14 -

R.A.G.E.

THEN I looked toward the sky and saw something. My eyes were still partially blinded but it was something I realized had been there all along, hovering just beyond the blurry boundaries of my awareness. It had purposely stepped out of the shadows and into the spotlight of my awareness.

Everyone else looked up and saw the same thing at the same time. More and more crafts appeared. Not machines. Not ships or planes or even EEMOs. They just faded into appearance and were hovering over us. Then, the first craft revealed what was inside — a grey! A grey — an alien creature in the... Flesh? Just as the pictures portrayed.

An energy jet shot out of the craft at a cluster of dragons, instantly vaporizing about a dozen. A warthog moved in for the kill and fired its tank zipper at the craft but it too was easily dispatched. The lead grey projected itself onto our screens.

"We were summoned to help our kind," communicated the grey.

Okay! I thought. 'It was nice knowing you all!'

Suddenly, another craft immediately zipped in from above. This one was dark and translucent but seemed more like a human invention. It fired its own ray at one of the grey crafts and destroyed it in retaliation. Craft for craft. Life for life.

"So were we!" said an unfamiliar but definitely human voice.

I looked at V-VIDS and saw the newest arrivals identified as Regulators Against Geostatic Extraterrestrials or R.A.G.E. The person speaking was the super cocky and confident Captain (Capt.) Felipe 'Flipper' Fernandez.

More and more R.A.G.E. units zipped in and stood by at the ready. The greys stopped shooting. Had they met their match?

And just as they faded in, they started fading out.

"We will be here," communicated the lead grey.

"So will we," said Capt. Fernandez.

"Thanks, Flip," said Young.

"Don't mention it, Quentin," said Capt. Fernandez. "We're always here for you little buddy." And just like the greys, the R.A.G.E. units zipped out.

"When Teresa told the General we had underestimated the Chupacabras, I knew it was time to call in reinforcements," said Young. "R.A.G.E. is a special unit not more or less elite than the General's forces... were. Only that they, we are specialized in combating stupid, stubborn aliens who won't leave us alone," revealed Young.

"They helped us out at the end, but it was you who won the day. We didn't know what to expect, but your sacrifices have made an eternal difference," said Young.

"As did Teresa's," said Stevens.

"And the General's," said Portman.

"You know he didn't have to die," I said. I couldn't believe those words were coming out of my mouth.

"Yes, he did," said Young. "He was a warrior who was fighting a war he couldn't win and one he couldn't lose. The Chupacabra Kinscog was a gift to his legacy and their lost lives were their gifts to us. They all made a difference we will see for the rest of our lives."

I thought about Cmdr Hall's words.

I looked around.

Other than the scattered bodies and wrecked machines, I noticed that the landscape remained pretty much the same; broken rocks, jagged mountains, winding washes, gnarled trees.

I kept thinking.

Not long after that, the clean-up crew started rolling in from all directions. The ole' flood bit provided a good 48 hours to clean things up properly. The infrastructure would take longer, but then again, there is always work being done on the border. I suspected it wouldn't be long before everything looked as if nothing had ever happened there.

The scraps of the grey craft would be reverse-engineered as usual. The machines would be recycled; the bodies examined, experimented on and ultimately repurposed.

I paused for a second. Before I allowed myself to think about the long work still ahead, I thought about the casualties and the families of the fallen. Their worlds were shattered by the horrors of war. Their lives would never be the same. Those who survived might live the rest of their lives fighting the same battles over and over again in their heads and in their souls.

But as I looked past the blackened blast craters, past the scarred boulders on the mountains and past the charred saguaros of the Tohono O'Odham Nation, beyond the land and people that time forgot, I wondered, 'Beyond the Babos, had anything really changed'?

I thought of the greys. I was angry. Angry to learn that they had been there all along and that not one of us realized it. Not even with our V-VIDS and ultra-advanced technology did we detect them. We were clueless. Greys hide behind the curtains of perception, just beyond the realms of technology.

But still, I feel them. I've always felt them. I remembered. Just as I felt them that dark night when I was just a little boy, wandering among windy trees when they first whispered my name.

"Victor."

PARTIES INVOLVED

Friendly

Gen. Hector Delgado / Lieutenant - Scorpion

Quentin Antone Young - Wolf

Commander Gonzalez aka Gonzo

Cmdr. Sean Hall - Lion

Cmdr. Special Agent Teresa Hernandez - Scout,

Doggie

BPA Victor Diamante - Scout, Doggie

BPA Stephanie Stevens - Scout, Dragon

M. Turner - Doggie

Roy - Pilot

Lt. Col. Havoc

10th Mountain Division, and 101st Airborne

Divisions

Capt. Felipe 'Flipper' Fernandez - R.A.G.E.

VL85, aka Vic - AI

BPA McMasters - HPU

BPA N. Portman - Doggie

The Grumpy Operator

Enemy

The Oaxacan aka Chuco Malo

Chupacabra King

Chupacabra Sentinals

Chupacabras

Grey

Neutral

> Melina
>
> Sasha

Campers

> Zaden
>
> Willow
>
> Sable - F
>
> Emorie
>
> Banks
>
> Rayden - F
>
> Hawk - M
>
> Taylor - F

Arecibo Staff

> Sentient
>
> Lead Scientist
>
> Sovereign Scientist
>
> The Voice
>
> SpecOps Captain
>
> Sgt. Brown
>
> Mousey
>
> Red Beard
>
> Nikita
>
> Sam
>
> The soldier
>
> His buddy
>
> Kevin

Fat Todd
Feezy
Brimm

END FILE *** END FILE *** END FILE *** END FILE

ACKNOWLEDGEMENTS

I want to recognize my little fireside buddies who reignited my passion for storytelling. Your youthful art and brilliant imagination gave wings to my vision. To my wife who made this possible by gifting me the freedom to chase wild dreams. And my closest family and friends who are one and the same.

ABOUT THE AUTHOR

I was born of Arizona, delivered into the mid-seventies, between disco, Tex-Mex and outlaw country music. I dined on desert winds and played carelessly on asphalt streets and along the dusty alleyways of South Tucson. My education began with a fine public elementary school; actually, schools; many. And even though I was cursed to the worst high school, I was blessed with the best teachers.

After my education, I thought I needed a break. So, I took one. But that break almost broke me.

I looked toward the military but was still undecided. After my recruiter, Sgt. Chacon, called my bluff and conjured up a job where I could "write every day," I joined the United States Marines, effectively swan diving into the swift raging waters of destiny. That was, and still is to this very day, probably the most important decision I have ever, and probably will ever make.

After joining, I discovered exotic new lands, peoples, cultures and civilizations. Then, I graduated from boot camp.

One of the toughest choices I've ever had to make was leaving my now, beloved Corps. After, I followed up my illustrious military career with an exciting year in furniture sales. Looking back, I think that year was the break I had always been looking for when I was younger. I finally had my own money, my own place, my freedom and more importantly, experience. I was making money, friends and enjoying life for a change.

But even though I was becoming a success, I still felt like something wasn't right. I felt vulnerable, exposed and unprepared for what was coming, even though I didn't know what it was. Later, I found out I had just escaped the crash of 2008. Almost all my sales friends had either quit or been fired. While all that was happening, I was insulated at the Academy, starting once again, at the bottom, at square one.

Made in the USA
Middletown, DE
20 July 2022